Nicole  'Dell

MAKING WAVES

Interactive Fiction for Girls

Scripture taken from the HOLY BIBLE, NEW INTERNATIONAL VERSION®. NIV®. Copyright © 1973, 1978, 1984 by International Bible Society. Used by permission of Zondervan. All rights reserved.

Published by Barbour Publishing, Inc., P.O. Box 719, Uhrichsville, Ohio 44683, www.barbourbooks.com

Our mission is to publish and distribute inspirational products offering exceptional value and biblical encouragement to the masses.

 Member of the
Evangelical Christian
Publishers Association

Printed in the United States of America.

Bethany Press International, Bloomington, MN 55438; February 2010; D10002230

Nicole 'Dell

MAKING WAVES

Interactive Fiction for Girls

BARBOUR
PUBLISHING

DEDICATION

*To my oldest son, Erik, who is about to become an adult,
but has already proven himself to be a man. I'm so proud of
you and how you've learned from the choices you've made in your
life. As I write these books, I think of you and wonder how to
get my characters to the same point of growth and maturity
that I've had the priviledge of witnessing in you. I thank
God for you every single day. I love you, son.*

Chapter 1

A LONELY PORTRAIT

The picture had been shot only six weeks before; but the edges were already tattered, and fingerprints smudged the image. Kate peeled it from the scrapbook page for what seemed like the hundredth time. She leaned back to lie on the floor and raised the picture above her head in one fluid motion—the rotating ceiling fan made the picture wiggle.

Three generations of Walker women stared back at her from the photo. Her silver-haired grandma sat elegantly, unsmiling, in a high-backed brocade chair, and her mom stood just behind, grinning. Kate's sister, Julia, looked regal with her ivory-lace wedding dress fanned out around the group like a moat around a castle. She wore her brown, velvety hair swept up in an elegant clip, revealing her long, graceful neck. Kate sat at her mom's feet just outside the moat, her legs twisted to the side as she tried to remain graceful, careful not to touch the ethereal hem of her sister's garment.

Julia. She drove Kate crazy most of the time, but Kate didn't know how much she counted on her big sis until she had moved out. She didn't live too far away—about fifteen minutes by car—but far enough so they usually only saw each other on weekends when Julia had free time, which, for a young newlywed, was pretty rare.

Kate heaved herself up with a sigh and returned to her scrapbook. She flipped one page back to what she had been working on the day before. Her gaze locked on an image of herself with her best friend, Olivia. Pacific Ocean waves lapped the beach behind where they stood together, laughing at a private joke forever frozen in the photo. Kate smiled because the picture showed just how little they had in common. Kate stood tall and slender, her shape almost boyish. She easily leaned her arm down across Olivia's much-lower shoulders. Olivia's bright blue eyes contrasted Kate's sea green. Olivia had a deep tan, but an equal coating of sunscreen and freckles covered Kate from head to toe.

Kate wiped the tear from her cheek. Missing Julia hurt, but missing Olivia was a different story entirely. Forced to leave Oregon, where she'd lived all her life, Olivia had to move all the way to Chicago to chase her dad's promotion. It seemed so sophisticated—and so very, very far away.

Of course, they had promised to stay best friends forever. But Kate wasn't that naive. Only a sophomore, Olivia would meet other people, develop other interests, and move on with her life. Kate would just be stuck in Bethany, Oregon, with the same people she'd gone to school with since kindergarten. Everything stayed the same for Kate, except now she had to do it all alone.

Enough! Kate slammed the scrapbook closed. She really needed to stop the moping and do something with herself. Her mom wouldn't be home from her job for a few hours, so Kate decided to go for a swim. There wouldn't be many more opportunities as the summer drew to a close. The past few nights, Kate noticed that the night air held a hint of the approaching fall, which meant cooler water, too.

It's now or never. She pulled on her swimsuit, grabbed a towel, and headed off on the half-mile walk to the nearby lakefront beach. A nice long swim would do her good. *Oops.* She ran back into her bedroom to grab a sweatshirt for the walk home.

The lifeguards waved to Kate. She nodded a greeting as she tied back her unruly hair then waded out into Lake Blue. She hesitated as the waves came in above knee level. She shivered at the first touch of the water on her thighs, already colder than a week ago. With resolve, she gave herself a silent *one, two, three, GO* and took the plunge.

Pulling through the small waves refreshed her. Each time she turned her head to the side to breathe, she felt cleansed. With her head underwater, she didn't notice that she had no one to talk to or that no one wanted to talk to her. It no longer seemed odd to be alone. She felt normal. Just God and her—everything was best that way. So she stayed underwater for as long as she could. She swam. And prayed. And swam. *Ahh, freedom.* The cares of life a distant memory, buried at the bottom of the sea.

She went out about a mile along the shore and then another mile back, and stood to wade into the beach. As her head popped above the water and the fresh air hit her face, the world once again seemed as huge as the mountains in the distance, but she felt stronger. Nothing had really changed about her circumstances, but swimming always had that strengthening effect on her. Kate just wished she could swim all the time.

Suddenly an idea struck her. Why couldn't she swim all year round? She could join the swim team. She had probably logged around two hundred and fifty hours in the water this summer alone. It would sure be different swimming for a reason other than pure pleasure. But maybe if she felt like it had a purpose, Kate could love it as much as the lake.

There was only one way to find out.

She toweled herself dry and slipped on her flip-flops then trudged through the sand toward the road. She hurried toward home, hoping she'd have time to make a quick dinner to share with Mom when she got home from work. She kicked at the pebbles on the road and thought of her mom. Four years ago, she had taken a job after Kate's dad passed away. They needed the money. She didn't like being gone so much, and Kate knew she struggled with loneliness, too. She could hear Mom crying in her bed some nights. But now, it was time—they both desperately needed a change.

"Mom, I think I want to join the swim team at school. What do you think?"

"Really?" Mom dipped the corner of her grilled cheese sandwich into her tomato soup and took a bite, leaning over her plate so she wouldn't drip on her business suit. She looked out over their backyard, seemingly lost in thought.

Blinking rapidly as though to reset her thoughts, she blotted her lips with her napkin and said, "Well, I think a sport is a great thing; and you're a fantastic swimmer. I just don't want it to affect your grades or keep you from participating in other important things like the church musical—you do that every year." She got stern. "You promised me when you took a year off from choir that you'd still participate in the musical. When does swimming start?"

"I just checked. Tryouts are in two weeks. Practices would start the second week of September. And, Mom, you don't have to worry. I'll stay on top of everything." Kate tried to look convincing.

"Well, what kind of schedule are we talking

about exactly?" Mom narrowed her eyes, the skepticism evident.

"Practice would be every day after school until five thirty. There's a sports bus I can catch, which would have me home around six fifteen. On Saturdays, there's either a meet or a practice. If, by some miracle, I make the varsity team, I'd also have a ninety-minute, before-school practice."

"Wow, Kate. That's quite a commitment. Are you sure this is something you want to do? After your swim schedule, church activities, and homework, you won't have time for anything else."

"What else is there, Mom?" Kate dropped her uneaten sandwich onto her plate. "If I don't go swimming, I just sit around here by myself all afternoon." She gestured at the house. "I don't even crack my books until well into the evening anyway. I might as well do something constructive and fun. Plus, maybe I'll meet some new people." She pleaded for understanding.

Mom closed her eyes for a moment and then, without opening them just yet, she reached out and touched the top of Kate's hand. She patted it, then looked at her and nodded slowly, gently squeezing. "I know it's been a rough four years for you, honey. You've had to deal with a lot of loss. Seems we can't catch a break since your father died."

After a moment or two, Mom shook her head as if to clear her thoughts. "You know what? I think it's a great idea. You should go for it. And there's no need to ride the sports bus home. I'll just swing by the school on my way home from work to pick you up."

Kate's mood instantly brightened. "That sounds great, Mom. Thanks! Now I just have to make the team."

"Swimmers, take your mark!" The coach shouted from the side of the pool, her whistle at her mouth, ready to blow.

Kate, already poised atop the starting block, leaned down and grabbed the edge just like she had been taught in the training session. Being careful not to fall in, she waited for the next cue.

"Get set."

She pulled herself a little closer to the edge, arms bent, pulling forward on the edge of the block but pushing back with her feet, like a loaded spring.

"Go!" The whistle shrilled.

Kate sliced into the water with ease then

used her powerful kick to propel her as she angled her way toward the surface, careful not to come up too fast and break her speed. The instant her head broke the surface, she pulled her right arm from behind her and began to swim.

She swam with the same long, strong stroke she used in the lake, but the still water felt lighter and crisper. It was strange on her skin, but a welcome change. She felt as though she were flying through billowy clouds on a sunny day. Kate swam fast and she knew it.

Reaching the end of the lane, she grabbed hold of the edge and turned herself around to go back. She'd have to learn how to do a flip turn, but the coach had said that she'd have plenty of time for that. The turn cost her a few precious seconds, but she still kept the lead. Nearing the end of the lap, she tucked her head under the water and gave a final thrust toward the touch pad that controlled the timer.

She finished her tryout, removed her swim cap and goggles, then hoisted herself onto the pool deck before the next swimmer arrived back at the starting block.

Coach Thompson walked over. "Great job, um, Kate, is it?" she asked, checking her clipboard and pulling a pencil from her short, curly brown hair. She was shorter than Kate but her sturdy stature exuded strength and power.

"Yeah, Kate Walker." She wrapped a towel around her dripping body.

"Where've you been? Why didn't you swim last year? And how did you learn to swim like that?"

"I have always loved to swim, and I just do it for myself. I swim in the lake a lot. And I mean a *lot*." Kate shook her head to the side to release the water from her ear.

"I can tell." The coach nodded and smiled. "Come to practice on Monday. I want to play with some ideas before we make any decisions about team placement. Okay?"

"So, does that mean I'm not on the team yet?" Kate's shoulders dropped.

"Oh no! You have a place on the team. It's just where that I have to figure out. Your speed and raw skill is good enough for varsity. But your start and turns need work. So we'll just see if we can make enough of a dent in those to have you swim varsity. Deal?"

"Deal! I'll be here." Kate sailed away as quickly as she could on the slippery pool deck to the locker room. She couldn't wait to give her mom the exciting news.

Brittany and Pam, two juniors, had just finished rinsing off in the showers. Pam turned off the faucet and nodded toward the pool. "Nice swim today."

"Thanks." Kate's body clenched in anticipation of a conflict.

"I'm sure you'll be swimming varsity," Pam said with authority.

"You'll be Coach's new prodigy, I'm sure," Brittany agreed.

"Oh, I don't know about that. I won't get in anyone's way," Kate spoke quickly.

"No, Kate. From the way things look, we'll be in your way. Coach is going to have you flying before you know it. It's good to have you on the team." They both nodded and smiled warmly.

"Thanks a lot." Kate returned their smiles, relieved they were just being friendly.

While she finished up her shower, Kate heard her cell phone ring inside her gym bag. She tucked her towel around her body so she could dig for her phone. *Olivia!*

"Hey, Liv!"

"Hey, Katie-bug. How's everything?" Olivia sounded a little down.

"Well, I just got finished with swim-team tryouts, and I made the team. That's about all that's new here." Kate's voice trailed off. She wished Olivia could be there with her.

"Of course you did! You're an incredible swimmer. I can't believe you never joined before this. Why didn't you, by the way?"

"Oh, I don't know. Life, I guess. It always seemed like too much time, and I thought I preferred swimming for myself. But I'm getting a big rush out of this team-competition thing. We'll see how it goes as the season moves on, though. But hey,"—she hesitated, not wanting to let her friend down—"is it okay if I call you back later tonight? Mom's picking me up in a few minutes and we're going out to eat. And," Kate laughed, "I'm standing here in nothing but a towel."

Olivia laughed. "Okay, we can't have that. Call me later."

Kate slid her phone closed and dropped it back into her bag. Sadly, she realized that she'd have less and less time for talking on the phone now. She shook her head to clear the negative thoughts. She took her long, damp curls into her hand, wound them together into a knot and secured the entire bundle with a clip, swiped on some lip gloss, and applied a touch of mascara to her light lashes. Satisfied, Kate grabbed her gym bag and her heavy school bag, jogged out to where her mom waited in her car and slipped into the passenger seat.

"So, how'd you do? Did you qualify for a college scholarship yet?" Her eyes sparkled as the car door swung shut.

Kate buckled her seat belt and chuckled, hoping her mom was joking. "You never know, Mom. You never know. But for now, let's eat! I'm starving."

Chapter 2

NO "I" IN TEAM

Coach Thompson stood at the edge of the pool in her purple track suit and rubber shoes, dangerously close to falling in. She looked up from her clipboard and peered over her pink and purple reading glasses at the girls' swim team seated poolside on the bleachers. "Hey, this is a pretty good-lookin' group." She smiled and nodded as she looked across the rows.

"Okay. It looks like we have a pretty big team this year, and I'm really excited about what I saw at tryouts." She rested the clipboard on her hip. "I think this is going to be an exciting swim season if you each do your part individually to achieve great team results. Just remember, even though you swim alone, you're part of a whole. There's no 'I' in team.

"New swimmers, I want you to go to the posting on the locker room door and find your lane assignment." She tipped her head toward the door. "Then, go ahead and get into your lanes and wait for further instructions. Returning swimmers, you know the drill. The workout is posted on the chalkboard—go to it and have fun!"

Thirty-six swimmers in racing suits, goggles in hand, climbed off the bleachers and went to peer at the list on the locker room door. Milling around with their shiny black swim caps on, they looked like a bunch of eight balls rolling around on a pool table. Kate tried to get her cap over her thick head of hair—no luck. She pulled and tugged on that tiny cap—still no luck. Just as she secured it over one side and moved to the other, it rolled up and her hair sprang free. She considered swimming without it just as she felt a tap on her shoulder.

"Need some help?" Pam offered.

Kate reddened as she saw that Pam's luxurious blond hair had been tucked under her cap without any apparent struggle. "Please." She was desperate.

"The trick is conditioner. You should get it

wet first. Then condition it, put it in a ponytail, and wind it around the elastic band." Pam took off her own cap to show Kate. "Then, your cap should slip on pretty easily. Plus, if your hair's already wet and coated with conditioner, it won't get damaged by being in the chlorine for so many hours every day. But here,"—Pam pulled an elastic band from her wrist—"use this for today."

"Thanks!" Kate took the elastic. "I'm doing that conditioner trick tomorrow, for sure." *How cool of her to help.* She managed to get most of her hair tucked safely away and went to look for her name on the list.

"Kate," Coach Thompson called. "I almost forgot. Your name isn't there. I want to use this warm-up time to figure some things out with you, if you don't mind."

"Okay. . ." Kate looked back to the locker room door and the other swimmers. "What do you mean 'figure some things out'?"

"Hop on in here." Coach gestured to the empty lane reserved for warm-ups and cool-downs. Kate lowered her body into the water, trying to look like a pro by not showing any reaction to the temperature.

"I think it's pretty clear that you can swim.

You're really fast, and you have a beautiful freestyle stroke. I'm sure that your speed is going to improve even more as you start real practices, and I can't wait to see what we can do with your times." Coach squatted near the pool's edge and lowered her voice. "But first, I want to see how fast you can pick up flip turns and starts so we can decide if you're ready to swim varsity."

Nervous excitement buzzed through Kate's veins. She could do it; she knew she could. She listened intently as her coach explained the mechanics of the flip turn, and then she pushed off the wall. As she approached the opposite side of the pool, she glided in with her arms at her side. She tucked her chin and rolled forward. About halfway through her flip, she unfolded her body, just like the coach had said. Placing her feet on the wall, she pushed off. Slightly off center, one foot slipped from the wall so it didn't have the power it could have, but she rotated to her stomach and continued to swim. *Not bad.*

After about fifteen minutes, Coach nodded. "Okay, that's enough. You're going to be great. Go ahead and swim with the varsity girls in lane five. Just keep working on your flip turns."

Kate hoisted herself out of the pool.

"Thanks, Coach!" Could things get any more perfect? She joined her group and eased herself into the water, careful not to get in anyone's way.

Pam and Brittany, along with a few other juniors and seniors, filled the lane. Since Kate had no idea how things worked, she stood to the side and let them pass.

Brittany blew a dramatic sigh and exchanged knowing glances with a few other swimmers. "See that chalkboard over there?" She pointed to the back wall, rolling her eyes. "You look there to find out what our workout is. It tells you how much to swim, how to swim it, and anything else you need to know." She rushed through her explanation. "It also tells you the times. See the clock? If you're given a certain amount of time to swim and you get back here earlier, that's a break for you."

Kate repeated the instruction in her mind so she wouldn't have to ask again, determined not to earn another eye roll. "Okay, that makes sense. There are so many girls, though. How does that work?"

"Well, we all start out swimming in a line on the right side. If someone wants to pass you, they'll touch your foot or leg to let you know. Move over to the right as much as you can and let them pass. Also, watch for swimmers coming toward you on your left as they're on their way back. Got it?"

Kate nodded and put her goggles in place. *Ready or not, here I go.* She pushed off from the wall and glided through the water until she surfaced and started to swim. Within seconds, she could reach out to touch the feet of the swimmer ahead of her. She considered not passing, just to avoid making waves. But that wasn't why she joined the team. So she reached forward and touched her foot and then passed.

In just a few more seconds, she touched the foot of the next person and easily passed that swimmer, too. At the end of the lane, she did a flip turn just like Coach had taught her—not great, but it could have been worse. On the last length of the lap, Kate passed two more swimmers, which put her first in line.

Sandy Coble, one of the star seniors, said through labored breaths, "Kate, go easy, this is a three-hour practice. Don't wear yourself out in the first thirty minutes just trying to prove something."

"Good point. But so far I'm fine. Thanks." Kate knew they thought—or hoped—she'd tire out toward the end of practice. But, in truth, she'd barely exerted herself yet. By the time practice ended, without even trying to—or really even wanting to—Kate had proven that she was the fastest swimmer on the team. She sighed. They would all hate her.

"Kate?"

"Mm-hmm?" She turned to the coach as she toweled off her hair.

"Can I talk to you for a second?" Coach beckoned with her finger.

Oh great. Kate followed the coach into her office.

"You surprised me today. When you came out like gangbusters and passed everyone, I thought for sure you'd be worn out by the time practice was half over. But it looks to me like you could keep going. Am I right?"

Kate nodded.

"My guess is that you held yourself back a little to try not to get everyone mad at you. Am I right?" Coach peered at her over the top of her glasses.

Kate simply nodded again, not sure what to say.

"Hmm. Just as I thought." She rolled her desk chair away and looked at the ceiling, lost in thought. After a moment, she abruptly turned to Kate. "Okay, that's going to have to stop. You do your best at every practice, no matter what. Okay?"

Kate nodded again. She wished she would just open her mouth to speak instead of standing there nodding like a dummy.

"If you're up for it," Coach continued, "I think we can push you all the way to a college scholarship. I've never seen such natural talent climb into that pool." She gestured with her thumb out the office door. "I think we can take you pretty far if you're up for the challenge. But you'll have to put in the effort and the time. Everything will matter—diet, sleep, practice, everything. What do you think? Can you handle it?"

"Oh, I definitely think I'm up for it!" A fire lit behind Kate's eyes. She had joked about a college scholarship but never considered it a possibility.

"All right then, you get on home, eat lots of protein. Be here tomorrow morning at 6 a.m. for our varsity workout."

Kate hurried from the coach's office toward the locker room. Her bare feet slipped a few feet on the pool deck then, reversing her direction, she slid into the door frame of the office. "Hey, Coach."

Coach Thompson looked up from her paperwork and raised her eyebrows in a question mark.

"Thanks!" Kate spun on her heels and hurried away, not waiting for a reply. She couldn't wait to tell her mom about all of this. Oh, and she had to call Olivia and her sister. They'd be so excited!

Kate turned off her lights and set her pink alarm clock to wake her at five thirty the next morning. Her gym bag and school bag were already waiting by the door. She could just jump out of bed and go. What a great day. But her excitement had been clouded by the one dark shadow over the day's events—Olivia's reaction.

"Now I'll never get to talk to you," Olivia had whined when she heard the news. "You're a completely different person now. I guess it's a good thing I moved away."

Olivia had sounded lonely, and Kate wondered if life in Chicago wasn't turning out to be as exciting as they thought it would be. Kate decided to pray for her friend. But before she got two words out, she fell fast asleep.

Yawn. After two weeks of early morning practices and not getting home until almost six thirty from evening practices, exhaustion weighed heavily on Kate. And on top of the schedule, Coach pushed her harder than the other swimmers because of her potential. As much as Kate loved swimming and enjoyed her celebrity status on the team, it took far more out of her than she'd anticipated.

"What's the matter, Kate?" Pam asked when she and Brittany arrived at the locker room after school on Wednesday.

Kate tugged at the straps of her swimsuit. "Oh, I'm just beat. Practice today and church tonight. Then homework. Then practice in the morning. It's just a long day. I'll live, though."

Pam snorted. "Skip church. That's an easy one."

I love church. "My parents make me go." Kate busied herself in her locker. Why hadn't she been honest with Pam?

"Oh, I would hate that." Pam wrinkled her nose.

"It's not so bad." Changing the subject away from church and back to the point, Kate said,

"Besides, it's only a tiny part of the reason why I'm so exhausted."

"Try a cup of coffee in the morning. It'll give you energy for practice."

"Ewww. I hate coffee." Kate wrinkled her nose.

"No one really likes it at first, silly." Pam laughed and pulled her suit on. "They just need it. You have to make it taste good."

"Yeah," Brittany jumped in. "I hated coffee at first. Then I figured out just how much milk and sugar to add, and now I can't live without it."

"Yeah, I guess I could try it." Kate shrugged.

Pam waved her hand. "Oh, just doctor it up. You'll get used to it sooner than you think."

"Mom, can you show me how to set the timer for the coffeepot?" Kate asked after church that evening.

"Coffee? Since when do you drink coffee?"

"It just sounds good for the morning before swim practice—warm, caffeine, energy. You know." Kate held up the can of ground coffee and the pack of filters.

"Well, first you make sure the clock is set correctly or it won't go off at the right time—

every time we have a power surge, it resets the clock. . . . See?" She adjusted the clock to the right time. "Then you measure out two scoops of coffee—well, I use two scoops and that makes me half a pot. So we'll use four scoops and share it." Mom scooped the coffee into the filter. "Then you add a pot of water right here,"—she filled the water reservoir—"turn it on, and you're done."

"Thanks, Mom." Kate gave her a quick kiss. "I've got to run—studying to do."

After what seemed like only minutes had gone by, Kate lifted the heavy social studies textbook from her chest and rubbed her eyes, trying to focus on the clock. Three in the morning. She rolled over to the side of the bed, let her books slide to the floor, and turned off her light. She pulled her covers around her fully dressed body and immediately fell back to sleep.

Riiiiiing! Kate jolted awake to the sound of her alarm clock. She groaned. *Five thirty, already?* Like a zombie, she climbed out of bed and stumbled to the bathroom where she splashed cold water on her face. Not yet awake, she made her way to the kitchen where she fixed a steaming travel mug of coffee with lots of milk and sugar.

Kate blew away the steam and took a

small sip. . .and then a second sip, finally understanding why people drank the stuff. It barely tasted okay, but its warmth comforted her tired and cold body and even the smell perked her up.

Later, in the locker room, Kate struggled into her cold suit which still dripped from the evening before, rubbed some conditioner into her dampened hair, and pulled on her swim cap. She took a final swig from her brew and felt ready to face the day.

"Wake up, silly! Can't you stay awake long enough to talk to your long-lost sister?" Julia's voice, a cavernous echo.

"Hmm?" Kate lurched upright. She'd crashed on the couch after practice got canceled, confused for just a minute. "Oh, hey, Jules!" She rubbed the sleep from her eyes. "What are you doing here?"

"I'm taking you and Mom to dinner. Surprise!"

"Cool! Does Mom know?"

"Nope, not yet. But we're leaving as soon as she gets home, so hurry up and get ready. Wear something nice," Julia added as Kate took the stairs two at a time.

Kate stood at her closet door and considered her wardrobe, hoping to find something more interesting than her beloved Oregon State University sweatshirt or one of her many track suits. She settled on a pair of new dark-wash jeans and an emerald green sweater. She even styled her hair with a blow dryer to smooth her frizz into silky waves.

"This is such a nice treat—having my two girls all to myself like this," Kate's mom said as she dipped a chip into the salsa at their favorite authentic Mexican restaurant. "And we don't even need an occasion."

"Well, actually, I do have some news." Julia sat back in her chair and grinned.

Kate and her mom both put their napkins down and swallowed simultaneously. Kate took a swig of water before she asked, "You're not moving away, are you?"

"Nope. It's nothing bad." Julia clearly enjoyed keeping them in suspense.

"You're killing us. What's going on, Jules?" her mom demanded.

"Well. . ." She paused, letting their

anticipation build. "I'm going to have a baby." She sat back and watched their reactions. In shock, no one spoke. "You're going to be a grandma." Julia looked at Mom, whose eyes were wide open as the news registered. "And you"—she pointed to Kate—"are going to be an aunt."

"Seriously?" Kate squealed in excitement.

"Oh, honey! That's wonderful!" Mom found her voice. She got up and ran around the table to hug her daughter. "I'm so excited!"

"Me, too, Mom. So is Kyle. It's a big surprise—we were going to wait a couple of years—but there's no better surprise than this." Julia twisted her napkin and then continued, her voice lowered almost to a whisper, "Boy or girl, I want to name the baby Casey. . .after Dad."

Mom gasped, overcome by emotion. "I th– think that's a beautiful idea."

Kate watched as Mom went through the stages of emotion that had been evident in her eyes many times since Dad died. Joy. Loneliness. Sadness. And then back to joy. When Mom could finally speak again, she said, "C–Casey. It's as it should be."

Chapter 3

CATCH UP

"So, talk to me, Kate. What's happening with you these days? I feel like I hardly see you anymore." Mom kept her eyes on the winding road and adjusted the visor to shield from the blinding morning sun.

"I know what you mean." Kate took a sip from her travel mug. "We used to have a lot more time to hang out."

"Right. I don't know anything about your new friends on the swim team, about your coach. . .if there are any boys you think are cute. . . ."

"Mom!" Kate loved to confide in her mom, but every girl had her limit.

"Well, okay, aside from the boy talk, let's catch up after church today, okay? We'll go to lunch, just you and me." She glanced at Kate.

"Sounds great, Mom." Kate slid down in her seat, hoping to nap for the rest of the twenty-minute drive through the mountains to their church.

Kept awake by the caffeine, she just watched the beautiful scenery pass by her window. Her mind wandered to the events of the past few weeks. Much had changed for her, but she hadn't considered how those changes had affected her mom. Of course Mom was even more lonely now than she had been—why hadn't Kate seen that?

There were no more hot dinners waiting for her after work that they could linger over while they talked about the day. Now they just rushed into the house, threw something together, and ate in a hurry so Kate could disappear to do her homework. She had morning and Saturday practices, too—so no puttering around the kitchen on a lazy Saturday morning, no stopping for a bagel on the way to drop Kate off at school, no more late Friday-night movie rentals with a big bowl of popcorn.

The image of her mom walking around the house alone haunted Kate's imagination. She promised herself that she'd make an effort to spend more time with her—time like they used to spend together. While Dad had been sick, they'd grown especially close and bonded over his care. Then he left. Gone. Kate only hoped that one day she could find the kind of love her mom and dad had—even though it hurt so much when it was stripped away.

She smiled and shook her head at her predictable mom, gripping the steering wheel and leaning forward toward it, bouncing to the beat of the song on the radio. How could Mom be so happy when the greatest love of her life had been taken from her? She went from having it all to being alone. Yet she seemed happy.

Once at the entrance to the church, they waited in line just to enter the crowded parking lot. Mom groaned. "It's getting more and more difficult to find a space on Sundays if you're not here an hour before service." She shook her head and turned down one of the last rows of parking spaces. "They're going to have to expand the parking lot again—they'll need a shuttle service like they have at the airport." She went up one row and down the next with no luck. She threw her hands up in the air in exasperation and shrugged her shoulders toward Kate. Finally, she gave up her search and pulled the car into the grass at the far end of the lot. As soon as she did, other cars filed into the grass behind them.

As they made the long walk toward the church, Kate twirled in a circle and gestured at all the parked cars. "Who'd have thought this many people would be beating down the doors to get into church? I guess that's a good thing, though."

"That's true." Mom nodded. "Good way to put it into perspective, Kate. I guess I shouldn't complain."

They reached the side door where a waiting usher handed them a program and took them to a pair of open seats against a side wall. Sometimes the enormity of her church felt impersonal to Kate. But when they visited other churches, none of them felt like home.

The purple curtain began its slow, billowy ascent to the thirty-foot ceiling just as the band started playing soft music. As the drape lifted, revealing more of the stage, the music got louder. A massive choir, in their amethyst robes with gold braiding, stood across the back of the stage on risers, swaying to the music. They opened the service with a rousing medley of familiar, old hymns rewritten in a contemporary style.

When the people stood to their feet, the

theater-style seating made quite a racket as the seats popped into place. Kate jumped right in, singing along and clapping to the music, her rich alto harmonies blending in with the choir. In moments like these, she missed singing with them—after having been a member for five years. But, she reminded herself, there would be time for that later. She couldn't do everything at once, and a one-year break would fly by.

After the worship time ended, Kate stooped back to push down her seat and then reached over to help her mom—she never could seem to get the hang of them. While the pastor walked across the long stage, the white-haired couple in front of her turned to compliment Kate's singing and asked why she wasn't in the choir.

"Thanks." Kate beamed. "I have been in the choir before. I'm just taking a break for this year." Her voice dropped to a whisper as the pastor began to speak. "I'm still planning to sing in the Christmas musical, though." Even as she said the words, she wished she could take them back. She would love to add that to her time off. But she promised Mom that she'd participate.

"Shh, Kate. He's starting."

Pastor Rick opened his sermon with a thought-provoking statement. "The trial may be inevitable, but the misery is optional."

Kate shifted in her seat, thinking about what he'd just said. *The trial may be inevitable, but the misery is optional.*

"Sometimes life's twists and turns aren't always what we want, but we can't avoid them. We have to go through trials and pain in life. It's inevitable. But in the midst of those trials, it's up to us how miserable we become. We can choose to become bogged down in the mire of disappointment, fear, anger, bitterness. . .or we can remain hopeful and joyful."

Kate nodded involuntarily.

"Think of Paul and Silas," the pastor continued as he walked across the stage from one side to the other, involving the listeners in every crevice of the large auditorium and even looking into the cameras now and then to involve the at-home viewers. "Paul and Silas were imprisoned for their faith. They were stripped of every comfort of life and were in physical danger every minute of every day. What did they do? They sang. They praised God. They were filled with so much joy. Not because of their circumstances, of course—their joy came from the Holy Spirit, from within them."

He seemed to look into the eyes of every

person seated in that room. His eyes bore through to Kate's soul.

"Joy is a gift from God that we can open in our lives. Joy has nothing to do with our circumstance. Nothing."

He let that sink in.

"Jesus promises that trials and tribulations will befall you. He also promises that He won't let you face anything so difficult that you and He can't get through it together."

He paused again and moved to the side of his podium. He leaned one elbow on it, resting conversationally. "Now, I have a question for you. Could it be that He might allow something to happen in your life in order to force your attention back to Him?"

Screeech! Kate stopped short on those words. *Could it be? Did He strip me of my best friend, my sister, and my dad so I'd turn to Him?* She couldn't accept that God would cause such pain and upheaval just to get her attention. How could He work that way? That's not the kind of God she wanted to follow. No way. Kate could believe He would help her *through* a trial, but she'd never accept that He *caused* it or even just allowed it as a way to turn her focus to Him. *No way.*

Kate forced herself out of her pensive reverie

to hear the final chords of the last worship song as the choir closed up the service. She'd missed the last few minutes, so lost in her thoughts that she hadn't even stood for prayer. She gathered her things and hoped Mom wouldn't question her lack of focus.

Before she had time to look at her mom, though, Kate felt two cold hands over her eyes. "Guess who!"

"Hmm, the Easter Bunny," she teased, unfazed, turning to look.

In feigned horror, Mark grabbed his heart, pulled out an invisible stake, and fell back against the faux plaster wall. He slid to the floor and to his certain death.

"Drama anyone?" Kate rolled her eyes. *That Mark. Funny, charming, and always entertaining.*

"Ha-ha. So, what are you doing right now? A bunch of us are going to go for pizza after church and then hang out at the mall until tryouts at three o'clock."

"Tryouts? For the Christmas musical? Oh no! I totally didn't know they were today." She glanced to see if her mom had heard. Lowering her voice, she said, "Mom and I have plans."

Mom interrupted—apparently she

overheard. "You should go, Kate. That sounds like fun."

"Mom, you and I were going to hang out today. I can skip tryouts. I'll just sing in the choir for this year's musical and not audition for a special part. I wouldn't mind that at all." Kate pleaded for a reprieve.

"No way, Kate." Mom shook her head. "This is much more important than whatever non-plans we had. You'd have wound up being bored all afternoon after we had lunch together anyway. This is much better than sitting home alone all day."

Kate shot her a look. How could her mother not realize that she wouldn't want Mark to think she'd just sit home alone, bored? *Mothers. . .* Kate shook her head and smirked.

"Will you have a ride home, or should I pick you up?" Mom, oblivious to her recent blunder, pushed Kate ahead with the plans.

Mark cleared his throat. "I'll be happy to see that she gets home, Mrs. Walker."

"That'll be fine. Thanks, Mark." She gave Kate a quick kiss good-bye, squelching any protest, and slipped ten dollars into her palm before she made the trek back to the car, alone.

Kate sat on the tile floor of the entryway and leaned her back against the wooden door of the vestibule to watch the cars go by outside. What was taking Mark and his buddies so long? Ah, footsteps, at last. But they stopped on the other side of the door. She leaned forward to grab her bag and started to zip it closed when she heard her name. She paused in mid-zip and didn't move a muscle. They had no idea she sat on the other side of the door.

"Did you guys see Kate Walker sing? Does she have any idea how great she is?" Mark asked.

Steve chuckled. "You've got it bad, man. Does she even know?"

"I don't know what you're talking about, Steve. Kate's just a good friend. But that girl's got chops, that's for sure."

Steve and P.J. both laughed. Kate heard a slap—she pictured them high-fiving each other. "You owe me five bucks," Steve said.

Kate panicked. Frantic, she looked all around her with no idea how to get out of her current situation. She didn't want them to think she'd been spying now that she'd heard them talking about her. She could feel the heat rising to her face—sure that her neck had turned a bright shade of pink.

"Yeah, right. They have to go out on a date first," P.J. protested.

"Oh they will. I guarantee it," Steve assured him.

"You guys have a bet?" Before they could answer Mark said, "Oh, never mind, I really don't want to know. Look, I've known Kate for over ten years. She's like a sister to me. I just think she's very talented. Have you guys seen her swim? She's amazing."

In the momentary silence, Kate imagined that Steve and P.J. raised their eyebrows while they waited for Mark to dig himself out of that last statement. Even she could tell he was deflecting. She patted her flaming cheeks and wondered how she would get out of this predicament. She would be mortified if Mark found out she'd overheard.

Now or never. With the stealth of a leopard, she leaned over to the glass door that led outside and pushed it open. Just as it closed with a loud clunk, she stood to her feet as though she had just come through the door. Then, with her head held high, she opened the interior wooden door that separated them and approached the boys as though she hadn't heard them. But because she had. . .she'd have to sort through all of that later.

Chapter 4

JUST TRY IT

She didn't dare look back. She lost more of her lead with every single stroke. Had the water turned to mud? Kate's arms had never felt so heavy before. Rather than glide across the surface, her hands landed with a resounding thud on the water like when she swung the mallet at one of those amusement park games.

The unthinkable happened. She felt a flutter on her calf—the dreaded touch of the swimmer behind her. Her stomach sank to the bottom of the pool. First she saw a pair of hands pulling through the water near her face. She tried to speed up—not a chance. She just couldn't do it. The hands gave way to arms and then the top of a head. Who could be passing her? *Ugh!* It was

Pam—a very smug-looking Pam. Kate knew she swam better than Pam—or did she? Maybe everyone had been wrong about her.

She'd failed. She didn't want to talk to anyone or even show her face. She hurried through her shower and then rushed to her locker to try to get out of there before the other girls finished with theirs. She just wanted to go hide out in her classes until the afternoon practice. Maybe she'd even go home sick. She clipped her wet hair back without even combing it and shoved her things into her locker, but she didn't make it out in time.

Pam and Brittany, wrapped in towels, turned the corner down the row they shared with Kate. They got dressed in deafening silence while Kate shoved things in her bag and slammed her locker door. Pam sighed and looked up at the ceiling for a moment. Then, she stared into Kate's eyes and said, "Hey, Kate. It's no big deal. We all have bad days. Don't let it get you down."

"Yeah, I have bad days all the time." Brittany rubbed her hair with her towel.

"Listen. . ." Pam put her foot up on the bench and rubbed lotion on her leg while she talked. "I had a really hard time my second year on the team. I started to take my swimming more seriously, so I worked really hard. I was tired all the time and my schoolwork started to suffer." She grimaced at the memory. "My parents almost made me quit the team because I just trudged around, barely making it through the day." She put her leg down and started on the other one. "Eventually, I just had to find a way to get the energy I needed to get through everything and still perform well."

"Me too," Brittany said. "I had my issues when I first started, too. Over time, after you find out what works for you, you settle into a routine and everything gets a little easier. You'll figure it out."

"That's the thing. I don't know what to do." Kate plopped onto the bench, put her head in her hands, and blinked back the tears. "I feel so much pressure. My mom is pressuring me not to let anything slip. Coach is pressuring me to be the best. I'm pressuring myself to earn a scholarship." She took a tissue from Pam and blew her nose. "All of those are good things, but sometimes it's just too much when you put them all together—especially when I'm so tired."

"Tell me about it! We all feel those stresses . . .or at least some of them." Brittany slipped her arm around Kate's shoulder as they left the locker room to head to their first-period classes. "I tell you what, meet us out here before practice this afternoon. We'll share one of our secrets with you."

"I'll be here," Kate promised. Maybe they did have the perfect solution—only one way to find out.

"Here." Brittany shoved a shiny blue metal can, about half the size of a soda can, toward Kate. Kate's backpack slid from her shoulder to the floor with a thud as she took the can, inspecting the label.

"What is a Red Dragon? I've never heard of it."

"Oh, it's just an energy drink. It's totally legal, and it's sold in every gas station. You'll see, though, it's way better than just coffee because it has other stuff in it that makes the energy stick with you a lot longer," Brittany assured her.

"I don't swim without one." Pam looked around her on all sides and then lowered her voice. "It's the only thing that gets me through a grueling workout and still leaves me with enough energy to do my homework later."

"Hmm. . .really?" Kate wasn't sure she wanted to resort to such drastic measures. "You're sure it's legal?"

"Oh yeah. I mean, there's no way they'd sell it to me at the gas station if it wasn't, right?"

Kate narrowed her eyes, skeptical. "True. . . but then why do you have to keep it a secret?" *What would Mom say?*

Pam shook her head. "It's not that it's a secret. We just don't want it thrown in Coach's face that we use this stuff. She probably knows, anyway. It's just not the natural approach she'd like us to take."

"Yeah, you know Coach, she preaches about all that good stuff—diet, plenty of sleep, herbal tea. . .health." Brittany snorted. "But believe me, she's happy with the results even if she doesn't know it."

Pam narrowed her eyes. "And, Kate, there are others on the team who drink this stuff. We're not the only ones. Pay attention, you'll start to notice cans in their swim bags and on the bus. Just don't make a big deal out of it. . . 'cause it isn't one. Okay?"

"Okay. If you're sure, I'll give it a try. What do I owe you for this one?"

"Oh, don't worry about it. Go ahead and have it. I'm sure you'll be buying your own after this." Pam reached into her gym bag and pulled out a can for herself and one for Brittany. At the same time, they popped the tops and tapped the rims in a mock toast. "It's best to drink it fast, because it doesn't taste all that great," Pam warned.

"Thanks for the warning." Kate took a sniff and wrinkled her nose. "Here we go." She tipped back her head and sucked down the tangy fizz. They were right. She gagged a bit on the first drink but kept choking it down. She shuddered as she swallowed the last little bit in the can. They turned to the locker room and dropped their cans on top of the other three that were already in the trash. Almost late for practice, they hurried to change and get out to the water.

Within fifteen minutes, much to her surprise, Kate buzzed through the pool, even a little giddy. Her fingers tingled and her head felt lighter. She pictured herself swimming to Alaska—she might actually make it that far. Could it all be in her head, though? No matter, she was back. She sailed through the water with her usual ease, and no one got close enough to even think about touching her leg—what a relief that that had only happened to her once.

"Hey, Kate!" Coach beckoned her over to the side of the pool toward the end of practice. "Come on over here. You're doing really well this afternoon. Let's work on some speed drills. How about a race?"

"Race? Um. . .okay." Kate gave a nervous chuckle. She couldn't think of a better day to test her limits. Coach called for Sandy to race the 100-meter freestyle—Kate's favorite race—against her.

"Swimmers, take your mark. . . ." Coach readied her whistle while the girls pulled forward into their starting positions. "Get set. . . ." They tightened up their stance, perched to spring into the pool. "Go!" The whistle blew and off they went. Kate had the best start of her life. A thing of beauty. How was Sandy's start? She couldn't tell.

Kate swam with all of her might. She breathed on every third stroke and sailed into her first turn in what seemed like record time. The water cascaded over her head and through her body. She had never felt so alive and in her element as she did in those moments. As she continued out of her turn, she realized Sandy hadn't even arrived to the end of the lane yet. She had almost half a pool length advance on her. How had that happened? Instead of relaxing in her clear victory, Kate pushed harder.

Nearing the end of the swim of her life, Kate gave it all she had. With as much extra thrust and power in her strokes as she could muster, she sailed to the end and touched the pad in record time.

She ripped off her goggles and looked at the timer. She had beaten the school record for the one hundred by a little over two seconds. Kate and her coach looked back and forth at each other and at the clock, stunned, as they waited for Sandy to finish her race.

She floated out from the wall, trying to cool her body down. At least two dozen swimmers hanging on the lane lines had witnessed the momentous occasion.

"Good swim!" Sandy said.

Kate tried not to make a big deal of it. "Thanks a lot. You, too."

She heard her coach's voice from behind her. "Kate, can you come into my office before you leave the pool area? For now, though, go ahead and cool down. I'm sure you need it."

Chest heaving, Kate swam two easy laps on her back to cool her body down. She hoped this wasn't just because of that energy drink. She felt

like she had been under her own power, her own
skill. . .but how could she be sure? By the end of
her cool-down, Kate decided that she had just
found a way to tap into the strength she already
possessed. Ready to talk to Coach, she hoisted
herself out of the pool and made her way to the
office.

"Well, well, well, Miss Kate. Nice swim,
to say the least." Coach shook her head in
disbelief. "Something tells me you've got a lot
of surprises in you." She put down the papers
she had been shuffling through and turned
her chair to face Kate. "I want to know how
serious you are about swimming. You're a first-
year swimmer, a sophomore, and you've beaten
our school record in a practice. Unfortunately,
the time doesn't get recorded because it's not
a formally timed event, but things look really
bright in your near future."

Coach leaned her elbows on her thighs and
clasped her hands together. "Then, there's the
long-term future to think of. Kate, you have an
amazing talent and you just keep getting better
and better. What do you think of all of this?"

"I don't know. I mean, I love to swim; and I'd
like nothing more than to push myself. I'd like
to earn a scholarship and swim through college,

if you still think that's a possibility."

"A possibility? Do you understand that the record you beat today is eight years old?" Coach shook her head, as if hoping she could get Kate to grasp the significance of what had just happened. "If you can swim like that in an impromptu race after you already swam a full practice, just imagine what you're capable of doing at the Regional invitational on Saturday. If you come even close to a time like that, you'll definitely get some attention and the powers-that-be will start watching you.

"Here's what I want to do." Coach picked up her clipboard, and Kate leaned forward in her chair. "I want to have you swim several events on Saturday. Let's get in there and make some waves. You can swim the 100-meter and 200-meter freestyle races, as well as the freestyle leg of the IM relay, and the anchor leg of the free relay."

Kate panicked. "Um, Coach. . .Sandy swims the IM relay."

"Not anymore, Kate, not anymore."

Kate left the office buoyed by the possibility of her future but concerned over the pressure she'd face from the other swimmers. Not only would they be counting on her to swim at least as fast as Sandy, but they'd expect her to prove why she was a worthy replacement. She hoped her coach wasn't making a horrible mistake. Sandy would hate her for sure.

I'm going to need more energy drinks.

"Liv! We need to talk!" Kate shut the door to her room and sprawled out on her stomach across her bed, her cell phone in hand. "I have so much to tell you, and I need your advice."

"Okay. I'm all ears."

Kate took a moment to soak in the image of her friend closing her bedroom door before settling down into her beloved purple banana seat. Once the sounds of settling stopped, Kate launched into a monologue about her life. She left nothing out: Julia's baby, the tryouts at church, the energy drink that helped her win a proverbial gold medal at practice that day, a shot at a scholarship, and then finished it off with Mark.

". . .He said I'm amazing. Well, I guess he said I sounded amazing, or something like that . . .oh, now I can't remember his exact words."

"I don't need the exact words. I already know you're amazing. And I already knew he thought so, too. You two have been destined to get together. It was only a matter of time."

"So, you think I should let it happen? I mean, if he wants it to, of course. He hasn't asked me out on a date or anything."

"Yes!" Olivia laughed. "I do think you should 'let it happen,' and he will ask you out on a date for crying out loud. I guarantee it."

Kate remembered that Steve had said the exact same thing. "Okay. I believe you. But we'll have to see. I still feel weird about it, though. He's such an old and good friend. Maybe it will feel like dating a brother."

"Perfect first-date material, if you ask me," Olivia assured her. "There's nothing to worry about. It's all part of your life's inevitability. Just live it."

Kate laughed at Olivia's cosmic approach to life. "That's true. Okay, enough about Mark. What do you think about the other stuff?"

"It all sounds so incredible. You're living a dream. Are you able to do it all, or are you falling apart?"

"I did have a hard time for a little while, but I'm fine now. I think I'm getting my second wind." Kate thought of something. "Oh, Liv. I wish you could be here for the invitational on

Saturday. It's going to be so exciting—a lot of pressure, though. Coach says this is going to be the moment that everyone sits up and takes notice of this new swimmer at Sandusky High School. What if I crumble?"

"Yeah, you'll crumble under the pressure because that's your style, right?"

"Ha-ha, funny. But seriously."

"I'm sure it's unnerving. But you deal with stuff like that well—look at what happened today. Just do the same thing on Saturday. Boy, I wish I could be there, too. I assume your mom is going?"

They talked for almost two full hours while Kate watched the sun go down outside her window. She ached for her friend.

Chapter 5

ON THE ROAD

Reclining sideways against the window, Kate ducked to miss the balled-up towel that flew by. A sigh escaped her lips as she gave up and shut her geometry book. No use trying to study with all the racket. Slipping her book back into her bag, she drew out a Red Dragon to sip. Turning in her seat, she drew her knees up and pressed her shins against the vinyl seat back so she could join the chaos in the back of the bus for the rest of the two-hour ride to the swim meet.

She popped the top on her energy drink. *Thunk.* The vacuum released. Only two more rolled around at the bottom of her bag for later, so she took small sips to make it last. Was it just her imagination, or did she have to drink more to get the same effect now?

"Gross! I have to chug mine when I drink them. They taste terrible!" Amber, a senior, shot Kate a disgusted scowl from across the aisle.

"I used to think they were gross, but the taste has kind of grown on me. I like to drink them slowly so I can feel the energy building in me." She waved her hands in billowing motions in front of her body.

"Do you really think it has that much of an effect, though?" Amber asked Kate, looking doubtful. She took a sip from a bottle of orange juice.

"Absolutely. I even like to mix in some coffee sometimes."

"Hmm, I just don't think I get that big a benefit from them, so I rarely spend the money."

"Oh, believe me, I hear you on the cost." Kate rolled her eyes. "I have to use half of my lunch money in order to buy enough for the week." Mom better never find out.

"That's what we do, too." Pam spoke up from the seat right behind Kate, pointing with her thumb to include Brittany who shared her seat.

"Who needs to eat, anyway?" Brittany laughed, patting her midsection.

"That's what I'm saying." Kate joined in the

laughter, feeling the buzz already.

The bus brakes squealed in the parking lot of a gas station. When it came to a stop and the driver opened the door, Kate stood up and raised her arms high in the air to stretch. The three girls ambled toward the door past a few rows of sleepy swimmers who were just rousing themselves.

"Come on, everyone!" Pam shouted and clapped her hands. "Up and at 'em! Let's see some excitement around here!" A few girls moaned, one covered her head with a pillow, and another lobbed a wadded napkin at her.

In the gas station, Kate hurried past the rows of candy bars and chips, straight to the coffee machine. She poured a large steaming cup of coffee and slid it into a sleeve before the others caught up with her. She flicked three packs of sugar against the countertop then ripped off the tops of all three packets at once and shook them into the coffee, spraying granules of sugar all over the place.

"Hey! You're making a mess," Brittany complained. "Simmer down." She laughed.

Adding three tubs of cream, Kate did her best to make her coffee palatable. Blowing away the steam, she took a tiny sip. She wrinkled her nose and added another packet of sugar and one more cream to her cup.

After another sip, Kate said, "Ahhh. Now that's what I'm talking about."

About an hour later, almost to their destination, Coach stood in the center aisle to address the girls. "Team, this is an exciting day. For you new swimmers, as you're probably tired of hearing me say, this is our first event on our way to Sectionals and then State."

Kate moved to the edge of her seat.

"You'll be making a name for yourself and setting a standard for your personal season as well as for the team. Today's times count as records for the season. And"—she looked around the bus and made eye contact with each of the faster swimmers—"there's a chance that some records will be set today." She shifted her position as the bus swayed on the mountain turns.

"Some of you may feel that your contribution isn't as exciting as some of the other swimmers', but that's just not true. Take everything seriously and do your very best. Even if you come in last place for a swim, the seconds you shave off can make a huge difference for the team's morale.

"And for those of you who have your sights

set on some big personal accomplishments today, relax, go easy on yourself." She pushed her glasses up. "I want you to do your very best, but more than anything, I want you to have fun."

They pulled into the parking lot of the Oregon State Aquatic Center and the bus squealed to a stop. Kate stumbled getting off the bus, unable to tear her eyes off the massive building in front of her. Was this where she'd swim? *Wow!* Old news to the seasoned swimmers, they looked away, unimpressed.

The instant they walked through the turnstiles at the entrance, Kate breathed deeply, filling her lungs with her new favorite scent: chlorine. She could hear the staticky sound of rhythmic splashing as teams had already taken their places in the water, warming up for the day's events.

They walked as a team, maroon and gold duffle bags over each shoulder. Nerves set in and no one spoke as they headed toward the locker room. Kate paused at the trophy case. Did she dare dream that her name would be affixed to one of those shiny gold trophies one day? *Someday—but now I just have to get through today.* Her stomach flip-flopped, and her hands shook. She lifted her head, pulled back her shoulders, and took a deep breath.

Steamy air and the riotous clamor of voices knocked Kate back a step as she opened the locker room door.

"Where've you been?" Pam wondered, tucking her hair into her cap. "We're almost ready to go out to the deck."

"I just needed a minute. Wait for me, okay? I'll hurry." She didn't want to step out onto the pool deck alone, so she put her things in a locker and changed into her racing suit in record time. She hurried around the corner, hoping they hadn't left her. But there stood four of her teammates, leaning against the shower wall, waiting for her. As a united front, they linked arms and walked out together.

The bleachers couldn't hold one more spectator. They came decked out in team colors, their conversations blended into one cavernous roar. Standing to the left of the bleachers, Kate scanned the crowd for signs of her mom's red hair. She looked up and down each row at the families—children with their books and computer games settled in next to their parents, grandparents with their cameras on straps around their necks, aunts, uncles, friends, loved ones all there to cheer for someone special.

After several anxious moments, she spotted her mom's bright red hair in the middle of the third row. As usual, her mom had gotten into a deep conversation with a stranger. Her ability to draw people out amazed Kate. *Wait!* That stranger sure looked familiar. *Could it be? No way!* It was Olivia! "Olivia? Mom? Over here!" She jumped up and down, trying to get their attention.

Olivia flashed a huge grin. "Ta-da!" She stood up and spread her arms as wide as she could, one toward the ceiling and the other pointed toward the floor.

"What are you doing here?" Kate mouthed, astonished to see her best friend.

"I wanted to surprise you!" The noise almost drowned out Olivia's shouted response, so she cupped her hands around her mouth.

"Come here!" Kate demanded with a big grin and pointed to the pool deck at her feet.

Olivia scrambled over legs and bags as she made her way to Kate.

Kate wrapped her best friend in a bear hug. "I can't believe you're here!" She looked her friend up and down. "You look exactly the same."

"Well, you don't," Olivia said. She held

Kate back at arm's length. "You're all toned and muscular, like you're ready for the Olympics. I can't wait to see what all the fuss is about." Her eyes twinkled.

"Well, I'll try to make your trip worthwhile." Kate laughed. "Hey, speaking of that—how did you get here?"

"Oh, my dad had to come to town on business, so he let me use some of his frequent-flier miles. I'm staying at your house until Tuesday."

"Perfect! We're off school on Monday."

"I know, silly. I arranged this trip, remember?" Olivia poked Kate in her side just as the warning bell sounded the start of the meet.

"I'm so excited you're here." She turned, in a hurry to get to her team. "I've gotta go now. But meet me in the hallway outside the locker room after it's over. I hope you don't get too bored." Kate gave a teasing smile.

"I'll be fine," Olivia assured. "You just swim your heart out. I'm rooting for you."

"Swimmers take your mark. . . ."

Kate shook her arms to keep them loose for her favorite swim, the 100-meter freestyle.

An hour before, she swam with her relay team to take first place. She could still feel the adrenaline coursing through her veins—the Red Dragon surely helped with that, too.

"Get set. . . ," the announcer continued.

She bent down and grabbed the starting block, poised to pounce. In those last seconds before the starting gun went off, she made a mental list of what she needed to do to make this a record race and looked ahead at the serene water. Even though the pressure was on, the water beckoned, and she couldn't wait to swim.

Bang!

Kate sailed off the starting block and flew through the air toward the water. She sliced through the surface with ease. Already off to an amazing start, she swam with all her might, reaching like a little girl with her sights set on a cookie jar—just a little more. . .a little more. . . And she pulled through the water with strength even she hadn't known she possessed.

It came time for the flip turn. It still wasn't her strongest skill, and her foot slipped just a little, which limited the force she had for the push-off. But she pressed on. Relieved that the length of the Olympic-sized pool meant that a 100-meter swim only had one flip turn, she'd sailed through the hardest part. Home free.

One more length of the fifty-meter pool left to swim. She looked at the lanes to her left and, with the next breath, to her right—the water rested, undisturbed. No one came close. Still buzzing from her second energy drink of the day, she pulled from all the mental, physical, and spiritual energy she had. The buzz plus her adrenaline and determination—a record-breaking combination.

Lord, please help me.

She swam for her life. Her lungs seared and her shoulders screamed.

Stroke. Stroke. Stroke.

She felt the speed coming out of her fingertips like lightning and heard the crowd cheering. She absorbed their energy and stroked even harder toward the end of the lane. One last big pull, she tucked her head and reached out for the timer pad and glided into it.

She looked at the clock—52.33! She did it. She broke the record.

Triumphant, she pulled off her goggles and her swim cap and floated on her back for a few seconds to cool down, still basking in the cheers. One by one the other swimmers finished their races. They took off their goggles and stared at the race results, panting to catch their breath.

"Congratulations, Kate," another swimmer offered before getting out of the pool.

"Congratulations. . ."

"Good swim. . ." People milled around, and Kate lost track of who said what while she reveled in the congratulations that flew at her from all sides.

"Amazing."

"Congrats."

Kate exhaled, still trying to catch her breath, and smiled as she responded, "Thanks, same to you."

She hopped out of the pool to get some water and wind down in preparation for her next swim—she didn't have long. She dug through her gym bag to find the banana and granola bar she'd tucked in there for that purpose. Her hand brushed against something cold—her last Red Dragon. She wanted it badly but didn't want to show weakness by drinking it right there in front of the other teams and the spectators, and she had to swim again in less than a half hour. So it would have to wait.

Immediately after she finished taking second place in her third swim of the day, she picked up her duffle bag, slipped the strap onto her shoulder, and walked to the locker room where she laid back on the bench to gather her thoughts. Towel covering her face, she tried to focus by reliving every moment of the race so she could harness it and do it all over again in a little less than an hour.

"Hey! There you are. Everyone's looking for you. What are you doing hiding out in here alone? You should be celebrating!" Pam shouted.

"Oh, hey. I just needed some time alone to think." She noticed that Pam's maroon suit dripped water. "You just swim? How'd you do?"

"Oh, who cares? You're the star these days," Pam teased. Her voice didn't hold a hint of malice, but her eyes looked just a little envious. Kate knew she'd probably feel the same way—or worse.

"I'm sorry I missed your swim. I'm just trying to stay in the zone for my next two races. I don't want to lose any steam." Kate popped the top on her Red Dragon.

"Oh, believe me, I can understand that. Everyone's talking about you."

"Ugh. Just what I needed to hear," Kate groaned, taking a big swig of her drink.

"There's no need to be nervous. You're doing all the right things. You're staying focused. And you've already finished three races. Three down, two to go. Easy. But, hey, if you need a little extra confidence boost, take one of these." Pam held out a little pack of white pills. "They're just caffeine pills. They'll sure give you a zing."

Kate narrowed her eyes. "Oh, man. I don't know. Are they even legal?"

Pam assured her, "Oh yeah. Definitely. You can buy them anywhere without a prescription. Totally legal."

Kate recognized the pills as the ones her mom took that first year after her dad died. After being awake all night, she had needed some help functioning at work. Kate turned the sheet of pills over and read the back. If her mom had taken them and they helped her a lot, why not? She couldn't get mad if she'd done it herself. . .right?

"Perfect." Kate peeled back the silver foil backing of the sheet of pills and popped one out into her hand. "Down the hatch."

After her last race, Kate sat on the bench in the locker room. She held three blue ribbons and one red ribbon for the IM relay in one hand and a card with her record-setting time in the other. Her eyes flitted back and forth between her winnings. Which to look at first?

She shook her head to clear it and tucked her memorabilia safely away in her swim bag. She pulled on her track suit and tied her hair back into a ponytail and escaped the chaos of the locker room to go find her mom and Olivia.

"Kate!" Olivia came running down the hallway when Kate first poked her head out. "You were incredible! I can't believe how great you were!" She jumped up and down and squealed. "Four races. . .three first places and a new record!"

Kate and her mom just laughed while they waited for Olivia to get it out of her system.

"You're going to the Olympics!" Olivia grabbed her hands and squeezed them. "You could seriously be the best swimmer ever!"

"Whoa, whoa, whoa. I'm going to have to stop you there." Kate held up her hand and shook her head. "Incredible? Maybe. Great? Sure. Best swimmer ever. . .nah. . .you don't think?" But she couldn't keep the big grin off her face.

"Kate, you really were beautiful out there, sweetie. I'm so proud of you." Kate's mom beamed and hugged her. "All that hard work is paying off."

If only it was all because of my hard work.

Chapter 6

FIRST DATE

Kate and her mom stumbled through the door with their arms full of packages. Kate let her school bag and purse slide to the floor. She reached to help as Mom heaved the two grocery bags, the carton of fried chicken, and her turquoise leather purse to the countertop. Kate lifted her mom's purse and waved it in front of her face. She wrinkled her nose in disgust and raised her eyebrows at her mom before she lowered the purse to the floor.

"You're a funny one, Kate," Mom said sarcastically—usually she harped on Kate for that. She turned to put the frozen mashed potatoes in the microwave. "You're right, though. The bottoms of purses carry more germs than—"

"Hello, Walker residence."

"Did the phone even ring?" Mom interrupted.

"Shh," Kate whispered with her hand on the receiver.

"Hi there. It's Mark Hansen."

"Oh, hi, Mark. How's it going?" Kate turned her back.

"I was just calling to see if you wanted to go out on a real date with your ol' buddy Mark."

Kate laughed. When did he not make her laugh? "Ol' buddy, huh? How nice of you to ask. When were you thinking?" She picked up a pen to doodle on the pad of paper near the phone.

"Friday night is as good a night as any, don't you think?"

"That sounds great. . . . I'll have to clear it with my mom, but it should be okay. I'll talk to her, and then I'll let you know in school tomorrow. Sound good?" She smiled and flipped her fully doodled paper over to the clean side. Mom tried to step in her line of sight, but Kate wouldn't look at her.

"Perfect. I'll talk to you then."

"Thanks for calling, Mark. Talk to you tomorrow. . . . Bye." The cap of her pen flew off when she slammed it down on the counter.

She groaned. "Mom! This is exactly why I need a phone in my room or at least a cordless phone that will work in my room." She had an afterthought. "Or a cell phone package that I can use to talk to more people than just you, Julia, and Olivia."

Mom laughed and put the tomatoes in the produce bin. "No. Calls from boys are exactly why you don't need a phone in your room. What are you so upset about, anyway?"

"I'd just like a little privacy when I'm having a conversation instead of you distracting me by making gestures and comments to confuse me while I'm trying to sound intelligent." She slumped onto a stool and put her face down on her crossed forearms that rested on the cold granite.

"You don't need to *try* to sound intelligent, Kate. Besides, it was Mark Hansen, right?"

Kate nodded without lifting her head.

"I mean, come on. You've talked to that boy in person every week of your life for years and years. Why all of a sudden is a phone call something special?"

"Well, that's just it. He's never called before," Kate whined.

"Come on, Kate. Be respectful." She narrowed her eyes.

"Sorry." Kate sat up a little straighter.

"What did he want, anyway?"

"He asked me out on a date." The microwave beeped an exclamation point as Kate stared at her mom, waiting for her reaction.

Mom stepped toward Kate without closing the refrigerator. "What? A date? Really?"

"What, Mom?" Kate challenged her with one brow lifted. "Is it so difficult to believe that someone might want to go out on a date with me?" She gestured up and down her body.

"Of course that's not what I mean, Kate, and you know it." Mom sounded frustrated and tired. "I just wasn't expecting this so soon."

"What do you mean, so soon? I'm going to be sixteen in three weeks. Most kids my age have been dating for a long time."

"I understand that, but you're not—"

"—most kids my age." Kate had heard it all before. She jumped off her stool, and it screeched backward against the tile floor.

"I've said that a time or two, huh?"

"Yeah, Mom. You really need to get some new lines." Kate rolled her eyes and smiled, beginning to calm down. She picked through the chicken to find a breast, peeled the fried skin off with two fingers, and left it in the box.

"The thing is, I want to go out with Mark. I think he's great and if anyone should be my first date, it should be him."

"Maybe no one should be your first date." Mom took a seat on the stool next to Kate at the island.

Kate ignored those words. "I know you've always said that I had to be sixteen to date, but are you seriously going to hold me to a matter of days?"

"No. Of course not, Kate." She sighed. "I'm not unreasonable, you know." Mom took a deep breath. She pushed her untouched plate away with one hand and rubbed her eyes with the other. "You know, your attitude has changed lately—more agitated and irritable. You've been using a tone with me that I don't like. Let's get a handle on that. Okay?"

Oops. She'd gone too far. "Okay, Mom. I'm really sorry."

Mom nodded. "Now, if you want to go out with Mark, under certain conditions, it's okay with me."

Kate stopped chewing. "What conditions?" She tipped her head to the side and slumped her shoulders, sure she'd hate the answer.

"I want you home by eleven. I want to know

78

everywhere you are, even if plans change." She
pointed at her fingers like checking off a list. "I
don't want you to be alone in someone's home
without an adult. Always wear your seat belt—
and all the other rules that you already know."

"Okay, Mom. That's all pretty reasonable."
Relieved, she came back with a cheeky com-
ment and a twinkle in her eye. "For now."

"Boy, you sure are a funny one, aren't you."
Mom swatted her on the behind as Kate
squeezed past her with their garbage.

"How did this happen so fast? You're not
ready for this," Mom mumbled as she left the
kitchen. "Come to think of it, neither am I."

"So, where are we going?" Kate asked Mark as
he looked in the rearview mirror.

"It's a surprise." He wiggled his eyebrows up
and down and grinned. "You look really nice, by
the way."

"Thanks." Kate ran a shaky hand down the
leg of her best jeans—a pair of comfy sweats
was more her style. Whoever thought denim
was a good idea, anyway? She crossed her legs
at the knee then uncrossed them and fluffed
her hair which she had worked on for almost an

hour. She took a deep, steadying breath—she didn't have to be nervous with Mark, so why couldn't she calm her racing heart? "So, come on, where are we going? What could be the big surprise? And Mom made you tell her. So, let's have it. . .out with it."

"It's not that big a deal. I just don't think you've ever been there before, and I think you'll really like it." Mark grinned with secrecy. "And . . .we're here." He pulled into the parking lot of a small, plain brick building with no window or signs.

"It looks like an abandoned warehouse." Kate knitted her eyebrows and squinted to peer closer.

"Well, it used to be a warehouse, but it certainly isn't abandoned." He turned the car off and winked at Kate. "Let's go. You're going to love this."

The car doors slammed shut, and Mark set the lock. Kate counted six other cars in the parking lot, but no people in sight.

He started to walk toward the building but must have noticed her hesitation. "It's okay, Kate. Trust me. Really."

Her shoulders relaxed, and Kate laughed off her trepidation. "Oh, I'm fine. Just trying to figure this place out."

Mark opened the door for her to enter ahead
of him. She stepped around him and walked
through the doorway, pausing to allow her eyes
to grow accustomed to the darkness. The heady
smell of rich coffee beans wafted through the
air—she took a deep breath, inhaling the aroma.
The bottoms of her feet tingled from the thump
of the steady drumbeat and bass rhythm that
traveled through the floorboards. She patted
her hip in time with the music, warming up
to the place as Mark guided her past a set of
restrooms, through the carpeted vestibule, and
past a red velvet curtain into what appeared to
be a bar of some sort.

Her eyes finally adjusting to the dark, Kate
could make out little round tables in the center
with their chairs positioned so their occupants
could see the stage. Each table had three votive
candles in the center and a menu with PERKIES
on the front. Around the outside edges of the
main floor sat clustered groups of overstuffed
chairs and love seats where people could relax
in a more comfortable and intimate setting. She
looked but couldn't find a bar anywhere. Loud
music already blared out of the huge speakers
as though they expected a huge crowd, but only

five of the tables had occupants.

"Let's sit over here, okay?" Mark put his hand on her elbow and steered her across the room.

Kate pointed to one of the stuffed-chair clusters away from the giant speakers where they'd still be able to talk.

"What a neat little place! How did you find this?" Kate asked as they sank into their chairs. "How cool to have live music at a place that isn't actually a bar. I never would have thought something like this existed."

"I don't think you've actually figured out just how neat it is just yet. It'll hit you in a minute." Mark smiled, his eyes twinkling.

A waitress approached their table and opened the little menus for them. "Can I get you two anything?"

"Sure. . .I'll have a. . ." Kate looked the menu up and down. "A café mocha sounds great."

"There's hope for the hopeless, rest for the weary. . . ," came the deep, raspy voice from the speakers.

Kate's ears perked up at the words to the song. She leaned in and listened, sure they sounded familiar to her.

"Cry out to Jesus. . . ."

Confused, Kate furrowed her eyebrows and

looked at Mark. "This is one of my favorite songs. . . . It's Christian music?"

"Yep, it's a Christian coffeehouse. It's all Christian music."

"How cool! How is it I've never heard of this place?" She picked up the menu and read the name.

"It's pretty new. They just converted it over from an old warehouse, and word is just now getting around. I'm helping them with their marketing a little bit by going to some of the area churches and passing out flyers to the youth ministers and pastors. I really hope that people will come out and support this place so it can stay in business."

"What a great idea for a hangout. I'm so glad you brought me here."

He sat back in his chair and tapped his foot to the music, a pleased smile spread across his face.

"So how do they pick the bands?" Kate asked him after they listened for a little while.

"Funny you should ask. . ."

Uh-oh! She'd seen that glint in his eyes before. He had something up his sleeve. "Oh boy, here it comes." Kate laughed good-naturedly and shook her head, used to his dramatic ways.

"The bands here don't get paid, and there aren't a whole lot of good Christian bands in the area, so they will pretty much let anyone who wants to get involved just take an evening and run the entertainment. When they don't have a band, there's recorded music, but you can imagine that the place loses its cool vibe when that happens."

"You're right. The live music really makes a big difference." She tipped her coffee cup to drain the last drops.

"So, I was thinking,"—Mark gave her one of his drop-dead smiles—"what if we put together a little group and played here once a month or so?"

Kate sat up straighter, intrigued. "I don't know. . . . What did you have in mind?"

"Well, you would sing, obviously. I'd play rhythm guitar. We'd have to get Ty to play drums and Gabe on bass. Maybe we could even get P.J. on keyboard, but we could do it even if we didn't have a keyboard."

"Hmm. Well, it sure sounds interesting. It could be a lot of fun. We'd have to get together and practice to see if we'd sound okay."

"With that lineup, we couldn't help but sound great." Mark exuded complete confidence without a hint of boasting. "But you're right. So, what are you doing Sunday after church?"

Kate laughed and waggled a finger at him. "You have this set up already, don't you?"

Mark hung his head in mock shame then chuckled.

"I guess I'm practicing with you guys after church. But. . ." Kate hesitated as she thought of her schedule. "I won't be able to get too involved in anything like that until December. My swim schedule is about to get really intense over the next month up through the State competition—assuming I qualify, of course."

Mark rolled his eyes at her humbleness. "Of course you will. But whatever works for you is what we'll do."

"So maybe we should look at starting to practice in December but not try to play here until after the New Year."

"That sounds reasonable. But let's see how it goes on Sunday. We'll just have some fun for an hour or two—no pressure—and then I can drive you home."

It did sound fun. But she tried to imagine squeezing another thing into her already-full schedule. She would go to practice with them on Sunday, but that didn't mean she'd do it for sure. *I can say no. It's easy.*

When the waitress came back to see if they wanted something else, Kate said, "Sure, that's enough mocha for me, though. I'll have a regular coffee this time."

"Oh, not me." Mark shook his head. "I'd be up all night long. Decaf for me, please."

The rest of the evening passed much like the first part had. They laughed, teased, and enjoyed the music like old friends. Surprised, Kate realized that she really enjoyed talking with Mark and laughed more in that evening than she had in a year. . .or more. Kate felt very lucky to have been around through Mark's transformation from goof-off to growing-up. She couldn't wait to see more. . .*much* more.

Chapter 7

TRICK OR TREAT

"Trick or treat. . .trick or treat. . .trick or treat. . . ,"
Kate chanted to the waves at practice the afternoon
of Halloween. A distance practice, no sprints. So
Kate got settled into a comfortable pace and had
plenty of time to think.

*If I do well at Sectionals, I'll qualify to swim at
State,* Kate reminded herself every five minutes.
For the next two weeks, she planned to put
everything else on hold. She would skip practice
for the Christmas musical—they wouldn't be
too happy with her, but it couldn't be helped.
She intended to turn down dates with Mark,
too—if he asked her out again. It had been
a week since their first date with no call. No
shopping trips with her sister—not that Kate

had called to invite her. Swim. School. Eat. Sleep. Swim. Sometimes the pressure felt like a crushing weight on her chest. But she wouldn't trade it for anything.

"Trick or treat. . .trick or treat. . .trick or treat. . ." She continued her strong strokes and stayed in her easy rhythm for the long swim. It felt very much like her swims at the lake. No whistles, no timers, no shouts from the pool deck, no starting blocks or flip turns. No one else.

Just me and my thoughts.

Olivia. It had been a full two weeks since she'd talked to her best friend. She hadn't even had a chance to tell Olivia about her first date. Olivia would be so disappointed when she found out. They had promised each other they wouldn't let distance come between them, and they'd still share all those special things. But the first important thing happened, and Kate didn't even call her. How would Kate tell her best friend that she had been too busy to pick up the phone to include her in one of her most important milestones? Olivia would be hurt— Kate could only imagine how she would feel if Liv did that to her. How could she make it up to her? She'd have to find a way.

Stroke. . .stroke. . .stroke. . .

Julia. Her baby belly started to show, so Kate had heard. She hadn't seen her since the night Julia surprised them with the news about the baby. *It's not my fault, though.* Julia just didn't come around very much, and she didn't come to church with them like she used to. Come to think of it, she'd never even been to a swim meet. But Kate knew she needed to do her part to stay close. She'd have to call her later.

Stroke. . .stroke. . .stroke. . . The soothing water washed over her head.

Mom. Time had served her well. Kate could remember when every single night, her mom would get ready for bed, close the door to her room, then break down. She must have thought Kate couldn't hear her. But Kate fell asleep to the sounds of her mom weeping more nights than Kate cared to count. Over the years, the crying jags quieted and slowed, and now they only happened once in a while. *It's been weeks. Mom's making her peace.*

Mark. Hmm. Kate picked up some speed when she thought of him and had to remind herself to slow down. She had a long way to swim and wouldn't be able to finish if she didn't pace herself. *Mark.* He really liked her—she had no doubt—and she liked him. But she feared that she didn't have the time to dedicate herself to the expectations of a new relationship when she barely had time for her old ones. She knew Mark understood her schedule, but did he really support her commitment to it? Time would tell.

"Trick or treat. . .Trick or treat. . .Trick or treat. . ." Kate cleared her mind of the heavy thoughts and slipped back into the rhythm fueled by her mindless mantra.

Dong! The broken doorbell chimed only the last half of its announcement. Kate's knees cracked as she unfolded from the couch. She put her biology book facedown and hurried to the door.

"Trick or treat!"

"Oh boy! What do we have here? Let's see, a princess, a cheerleader, a scary monster." A terrifying roar pierced her ears. "Oh my, how scaaary!" Kate shuddered, playing along with the kids. "And a ballerina, a dinosaur, and a pirate. What a great bunch of costumes, you guys!"

Propping the screen door open with her knee, she held out the candy bowl for them to help themselves. Chubby little hands reached out from their costumes and dug in the bowl for the perfect piece of candy. Each child only took one, so she whispered, "Go ahead, take two, just for being so cute and polite."

"Thank you!" They hopped off the porch step and ran to their waiting parents. "She gave us two, Mom," she heard several say.

One after another, the parade of children continued through the evening. By nine o'clock, the steady flow of kids had slowed to a trickle.

When the phone rang, Kate checked the caller ID. "Hey, Mom. I need to take this. Can you man the door?"

Mom put her magazine down on the arm of the recliner and gave a mock salute. "I'm on it."

Stepping into the kitchen for privacy, Kate answered the phone. "Hey, Mark. What's going on?"

"Nothing much here. How about you?"

"Oh, we're just having fun with the little trick-or-treaters. Have you had many?" Kate peeked out into the family room to make sure Mom couldn't hear her and then sat on one of the kitchen stools.

"Well, my parents don't want to support Halloween because of its pagan roots and all that. So we just keep our front lights off, and the kids don't come here."

"Oh man, I would hate that. I love seeing

their cute little costumes. And they don't mean anything bad by it." Kate reached for the doodle pad and pen.

"Oh, I know they don't, and they definitely are cute. I'm not really sure how I feel about the whole thing. But I guess I can agree with my parents that it's best not to further any darkness when it's something you can avoid."

"So are you saying that if you had kids, you wouldn't let them wear a costume to school?" She doodled a jack-o'-lantern with question marks for eyes.

"Hmm, I hadn't thought of that." He paused for a second. "You know, I don't think I'd go that far. But I sure wouldn't let them dress up as anything evil like witches or ghosts. You know?"

"Sure, I think that's gross when kids do that anyway. They're little kids. They should be princesses and superheroes."

"Right." For several moments Kate listened to the dead air, wondering if Mark was going to speak. Should she say something?

"Well, now that we've got that settled. . ." Mark broke the awkward silence, and they both laughed.

"You mean that's not why you called?" Kate teased.

"Um. . .no. . .although it was interesting.

The real reason I'm calling is to see what you're doing this weekend. Want to go out to a movie on Friday night?"

Kate groaned. "Oh, you're tempting me. I promised myself I wouldn't do anything but swim, eat, sleep, and go to school until after the State championships." She made a quick decision. "But I suppose a movie won't set me back much."

"Good! You've still got to have a life. I promise I'll have you home early."

"Well, this is my life right now." Kate chuckled. *Take it or leave it.*

"Score!" Mark hooked the empty popcorn carton into the trash.

"That was a decent movie," Kate said as she stepped through the movie theater door that Mark held open for her.

"I'll go with decent, but probably not much more than that. Definitely not a re-watcher." He put his hand on the small of her back as they walked through the parking lot.

A nervous shiver ran through Kate's body as she felt his touch.

"You cold?" He pulled her closer.

How do I let him know that this is not a first-kiss night? Or is it?

"Want to go to Perkies for a cup of decaf and to check out the band?"

Kate looked at her watch. Plenty of time. "Sure, I'm up for that."

Once they had settled into their favorite overstuffed chairs, Mark ordered a decaf mocha.

Kate said, "I'll have a large, no foam, extra whip, sugar-free vanilla latte with an extra shot." She laughed at Mark's chin that had fallen into his lap. "What? You never heard someone order coffee before?"

"Well, Kate, come on. You didn't just order coffee." He shook his head and chuckled. "You ordered a four-course meal complete with soup and dessert. In fact, you even told the chef how to make it." He laughed and then stopped short. "Wait a second. Did I hear you right? Did you ask for extra whip, sugar-free? Don't they kind of cancel each other out?"

The waitress arrived with their drinks before Kate had a chance to answer. She took a sip and said, "Ah. . .perfection." She sat back with a satisfied smile.

"Nothing wrong with perfection, I guess." Mark looked deeply into her eyes.

Kate broke eye contact by looking away. "I'll be right back." She grabbed her purse and went into the restroom. She didn't need to use it, but she needed to gather her thoughts. *I like him—how could I not?* She stared at her reflection in the mirror. *But. . .* Nerves nagged at her—it was happening too fast. *One thing at a time, Kate.* But she knew she could trust Mark, so, if need be, she could slow him down. For now, she decided she could handle the way things were going. Probably.

Chapter 8

REALITY STRIKES

After a hot shower, Kate padded barefoot down the hall toward her room, tightening her robe on the way. She hesitated, surprised to see her bedroom door open. Hadn't she closed it? She brushed off her concern and smiled when she saw that she had a visitor—Mom sat waiting on her bed. Kate's smile wavered a bit when she noticed her mom's somber expression and the swim bag on her lap.

"What's up, Mom? You packing me up and sending me away?" Her voice quivered as she joked. She bent at her waist and flipped her hair over to comb through her thick curls, trying to figure out what could be going on. Why did Mom have her swim bag? *Uh-oh.*

"We need to talk."

Hearing the seriousness in her mom's tone, Kate flipped her hair back over and sat down on the edge of the bed beside her. "What's going on, Mom?"

Mom fingered the zipper on the maroon and gold duffle bag. She took a deep breath. "Kate, I don't search through your things, you know that. I just wanted to put a few granola bars in your bag because I've been concerned that you're not eating enough. You're getting too skinny, honey."

Kate opened her mouth, but Mom held up her hand to stop the protest. "But that's not what we need to talk about right now."

Kate closed her mouth and waited.

"I found these." Mom reached into the bag and pulled out a small pile of caffeine pill packets, little bottles of single-serving energy serum, and four cans of Red Dragon—two full, two empty. She just stared at Kate.

She had to answer this just right if she had any hope of convincing her mom that she didn't have a problem. *But I can't lie to her.* She rose from the bed and went to the mirror where she picked up her comb and pulled it through her hair. *Be calm—stay casual.* "Mom, I don't understand. What's the problem?"

"Kate, these are addictive substances, like speed."

She shook her head. "No, they aren't speed at all; and they're no more addictive than coffee. Most people drink coffee every day. You can't start your day without half a pot, yourself. And this stuff won't discolor your teeth," Kate said, trying to brush it off.

"Kate, this is far more serious than coffee." Mom took several moments before she spoke again. "I have several questions, and I expect honest answers. . . . First of all, where did you get this stuff?"

"Oh, they sell it at every gas station, drug-store, grocery store—everywhere. I'm not sure where I picked up each item." Kate kept her tone casual, knowing the wrong answer would seal her fate. "Most of it came from the gas station by school, though. It's all perfectly legal, Mom. As legal as buying a cup of coffee." Still trying to diffuse her mom's concern. "By the way, I checked; there's really no more caffeine in these drinks than there is in a good cup of coffee. So, what's the difference?"

"First of all, comparing it to coffee isn't a great move, Kate. Coffee has three times the amount of caffeine that a soda does—it's not good for you regardless of how many people drink it. Including me. And caffeine is only one of the ingredients in these products. Here, look." Mom tossed a can to Kate as she read off the one in her hands. "Guarana, ginseng. . .do you know what those are and the effects they can have on your body? How about the other unpronounceable words on there? Do you know what they are? I sure don't."

"No. I don't know." *What does she want from me?*

"Do you have any idea what your heart rate is before and after you drink these?"

Kate shook her head and crossed her arms.

"Well, isn't it possible that the 'energy boost' involves an increase to your heart rate, which you wouldn't want to add on top of what an intense swim workout does to your heart? Right?"

Kate nodded. *Busted.*

"Do you know that kids have died from drinking these drinks?"

That did it. Kate held up a hand. "Mom, come on. Kids have died crossing the street or from choking on gum. That's not my fault, and it doesn't mean I shouldn't cross the street or chew gum, right?"

"But this is completely different, Kate, and you know it." Mom looked up at the ceiling as though collecting her thoughts. "Let me ask you, Kate. Do you only take one pill *or* one energy drink *or* one cup of coffee?"

"At a time, sure," Kate reassured her mom.

"Kate, I want you to level with me. You know I can tell when you're not being honest. I want to know how much of this stuff you take in a day. I know you drink coffee in the morning on the way to swimming. Then what?"

"I usually take a caffeine pill at school." Kate hesitated. Could she get away without telling her the rest?

"And. . . ? Then what?"

"Oh, I don't know. I don't keep track, really." Judging by the look on her face, Mom wouldn't let it go at that. And if she didn't give her mom the information she wanted, it would make the whole thing appear a lot worse. How could she say this without lying? "I take a caffeine pill at the start of every practice and then drink an energy drink midway through if I feel like I need it—you know, if it's a hard practice or I'm unusually tired." She almost added "That's it" to the end of her sentence, but that would have been a lie.

"That plus the half-a-pot of coffee you have in the morning equals. . ."—Mom did the math in the air with her finger—". . .anywhere from one thousand to twelve hundred milligrams of caffeine a day, not to mention the other stuff in that can. And that's if you're telling me the truth about how much you use." She stared hard at Kate. "But I'm concerned that you're understating the truth." She paused for a moment, rubbing the creases in her forehead. "Tell me this, Kate. Where do you get the money to buy this stuff?" She gestured in disgust at the stash of promised energy that lay in a heap on Kate's bed.

"Oh, it's just a few bucks here and a few bucks there. I don't know—my allowance, I guess."

"Tell me what you've had for lunch this week. And I'll be able to check the school cafeteria menu to see if it was on the menu that day." She shook her head and held up her hand, reconsidering. "No. That's not necessary. We have an honest relationship, so I think I can just ask you what I need to know and believe that you'll tell me."

Kate nodded, grateful. At least her mom still trusted her enough not to check up on her.

"So, here's what I want to know." She paused, staring into Kate's eyes as though willing the truth from them. "How many times last week did you skip lunch so you could buy energy supplements?"

"Twice." *Liar!* But she couldn't tell her mom that she only ate lunch once. Not only would she have a fit about the misuse of her lunch money, but she'd start in on Kate about her health again.

Mom pursed her lips and shook her head. "Well, Kate, that's going to stop right now. If I have to, I'll put your lunch money in an account at the school so you have no choice but to use it for lunch. I hope I won't have to do that, though—I'd rather trust you. And if you keep losing weight, I'll come to your school on my own lunch hour and sit with you while you eat."

"Okay, Mom. I promise. I'll eat a good lunch every day." She meant it but had already started doing mental calculations to find a way to have enough money to buy her energy drinks anyway. Babysit? Sell some stuff? Borrow?

"This has to stop, Kate. No more energy supplements, okay?"

Figures. But Kate wouldn't give up without a fight. "Mom, I promise that I won't ever touch

that stuff again once the swim season is over.
I have State coming up, and I really need the
boost."

The light dawned on Mom's face, and she
asked, "I hope your coach doesn't push this stuff
on you. . .does she?"

"Oh no! She has no idea. She wouldn't like
it, either."

"Good." She sounded relieved. "It's decided.
You're done. State or no State, I'm not having
my daughter pouring this garbage down her
throat every day. If you're under so much
pressure that you can't swim without this stuff,
I'm happy to let you quit the team." She stared
hard into Kate's eyes. "I hope you don't feel that
kind of pressure from me."

"No, Mom, of course not. I just really want
to do well." She pondered her situation and
paced across her beige shag carpet. "I tell you
what. I'll stop completely except for the day of
Sectionals and the day of the State competition.
Okay?" By clearing out her system before then,
the supplements would have more of an effect
on those days, anyway.

"No way. I want to go and watch you swim
knowing that you're doing the very best job you
can without hurting yourself. I can't support the

need to win at all costs. What kind of mother would I be if I did that?" She stood to leave, bending to scoop up the pile of contraband. "Kate, don't forget that you have power through Christ to not get sucked into the trappings of the world. You don't need this stuff." She gestured to the substances. "You can pray for strength, power, energy. He'll give you what you need if it's His will for you to have it."

"I'll try that, I guess."

"Prayer isn't something you 'try.' You're either committed to God's will for you, and then you surrender to it through prayer; or you don't trust Him, and you look to outside things. That's something you need to work out."

Mom stood at the door. "I know that teenagers use this stuff, and I know it's legal, Kate. But it's not healthy, and I won't allow it. I care about you too much."

Frustrated, Kate looked out the window in the dark backyard, watching her mom in the reflection on the window. *Mom won't be in the locker room,* Kate told herself. If she really needed help, Pam would get her what she needed.

Mom put her hand on the door frame and turned to add, "You're done with this stuff. I'm going to trust you not to go against my wishes on this. Don't sneak around, Kate. Our trust is strong, but it can easily be eroded." She left without another word.

Kate looked at her reflection in the window. How had Mom read her mind? *Oh, don't be silly, Kate. She was a teenager once, too. She probably knows you better than you know yourself. She's right, though. I haven't prayed about this at all— not for real. But I can't. I wonder why I can't.*

The next day, when Pam and Brittany went to the locker room for a quick shot of Red Dragon, Kate stayed in the pool to avoid the inevitable questions. She felt proud, even glad she'd quit. At the end of the workout, she had to admit that she hadn't craved an energy supplement at all. She had plenty of zip without them—maybe she didn't need them after all. The day after that, though—another story completely.

"Come on, let's go get you a boost of energy." Pam nudged Kate, who sat slumped on a bench, and motioned toward the locker room.

"I'm fine," Kate snipped, not even lifting her head off the concrete wall where it rested with the crook of her arm covering her eyes. She lifted her arm just enough to look at Pam with one eye. "I'll let you know if I need something, not the other way around. Okay?"

"Fine. Sheesh, Kate. What's gotten into you?" Pam looked like she'd been stung. "Are you getting nervous about Sectionals next week?"

"I'm sorry. I don't mean to be cranky. I don't know what my problem is," Kate lied and squinted through her blinding headache.

"You seriously need some pep in your step. Let's go get a drink." Pam turned toward the locker room but realized that Kate hadn't moved at all. "You coming?"

"I can't." Kate shook her head and told Pam the whole story with her eyes closed while she rubbed her temples.

"Oh, no problem." Pam waved in the air. "We can fix that. I've got stuff in my bag. I'll share."

"No. I can't." Kate sighed and looked up at the ceiling, trying to think of a way to explain. "First of all, I can't afford it. And. . .well. . .my mom and I have a trust thing. I don't want to break that."

"Well, don't worry about the money. I have all of my birthday money. I'll get you through the next couple of weeks, and you can pay me

back a dollar a week if that's all you can do."
Pam shrugged. "But as for the trust thing, come
on, Kate. No one ever does everything the way
their parents want them to. It's no big deal.
She'll never even find out."

"Seriously, Pam, I can't—the money is only
a small part of my reasons. The real issue is that
ever since my dad died, I've tried to make things
easier on my mom. Then my sister got married
and moved out this summer. So it's just me and
Mom." Kate shook her head. No backing down.
"If I disappoint her or break her trust in me, it'll
hurt me more than it'll hurt her, I think. I just
can't do it." She looked away, teary eyed. "She's
been hurt enough."

For a moment, Pam looked like she had
more to say. Instead, she just shrugged her
shoulders. "Well, it's your call. The offer stands
if you change your mind. I'll be right back."

Even though she had a headache, Kate
finished the rest of the practice as best she
could. She felt like she lost even more steam
about halfway through, but she didn't give up.
When the day ended, at least she could say that
she'd remained true to her mom's wishes.

She got dressed in silence, trying to
formulate a plan. She'd just have to really buckle

down even more and get plenty of sleep. She'd shoot for nine hours a night for the next couple of weeks and hope that the added recovery time would make up for her lack of energy support. But would it be enough?

Chapter 9

THE CHAMPIONSHIPS

Coach Thompson balanced in the aisle of the moving bus as she looked up and down the seats. "Team, this is a momentous occasion. But we'll talk swim stuff tomorrow morning. Tonight, just rest your minds and your bodies. Have fun, girls. Soak this in. This is the experience of a lifetime—for some of you, this is only a stepping-stone." She made eye contact with Kate. Kate nodded almost imperceptibly.

"Now, here's what's going to happen. We should arrive at the hotel in about five minutes. We'll get checked in and then head right over to the pool. Tonight is the diving competition. We'll all go together to support our divers."

A cheer erupted at the front of the bus as

the divers and their coach waved back to the swimmers.

"Then, it's early to bed. There will be no movies, staying up late, hanging out, chatting. This is the very last night that you can do anything to affect your performance. Please, don't throw it away because you want to party. Let's stay focused—for your own sake, for the sake of your team. Deal?"

Everyone nodded in agreement, their faces somber.

"Okay then, here we are. Let's go to it, girls."

"Let's see." Kate checked the list Coach gave them. "We're supposed to have oatmeal, fruit, and an egg-white omelet." She, Pam, and Brittany ordered the same breakfast and topped it off with coffee—not on Coach's list. They gobbled their food, in a hurry to get to the pool.

They jogged across the parking lot of their hotel to the sports arena across the street. The bowl of oatmeal sat like a heavy lump in Kate's belly, and the egg-white omelet didn't agree with her at all. Hopefully, the nervous rumbling in her stomach would pass soon. She took the last swig of her coffee and dumped the cup into the trash outside the women's locker room.

"Here we are, girls." Coach looked around the circle of teammates. "I can't believe the season is almost over. This is it. What a way to end it!" She made eye contact with each swimmer and then blinked her eyes several times.

Holding back tears? Really, just an old softy. Kate smiled.

"This is the first time we've ever had this many swimmers who qualified for the State competition."

Kate's cell phone rang in her bag and Pam, Brittany, and Sandy snickered. Without changing expression, she used her feet to shove the bag farther under her seat so Coach wouldn't hear it.

"Not only does this reflect well on me, your coach, but it reflects on each one of you. It shows the support and encouragement that you've all given to each other. I'm so proud of each and every one of you." She gestured with open arms. "This is a very special group, and each one of you is very dear to my heart."

Kate's phone uttered one last lonely beep to signal a voice mail message.

"Girls, you know your stuff. I'm not going

to spend a bunch of time telling you how to swim. If you didn't know how to work your meet already, you wouldn't be here. Just go out there, do your thing, and have fun!" The girls stood and cheered. Their energy sizzled with electricity. "Kate and Sandy, I'd like to see you two, if you don't mind."

"Whoops! We're in trouble, Kate." Sandy laughed.

When the others had cleared out, Kate said, "What's up, Coach?"

"Girls, you're both scheduled to swim four events. Unfortunately, Kate, two of yours are merely separated by three heats—maybe twenty minutes. That's going to be tough. Your other two races should be fine, though." She pointed at the schedule.

"I'll be fine, Coach. The two hundred is first—that worked well for me at Sectionals. And there's over an hour between the IM relay and the one hundred. I'll just have to get some rest in there. I'm ready for this." Kate nodded with confidence. Could they hear the butterflies fluttering in her stomach?

"Me, too." Sandy put up her hand for a high five, and Kate's hand met hers with a satisfying *slap*.

"I know. I can't wait to see how things go today. You two have really made this an exciting year. You and my new ulcer." They all laughed.

Right before she went out to the pool, Kate checked her phone to see who had called. *Olivia.* Kate groaned. She'd missed two other calls from Olivia in the past week. She probably just wanted to wish Kate good luck. It would have to wait.

She walked out onto the deck and stopped. People had to walk around her while she stood transfixed, unable to move. The sight of the crystal clear water, the echoing sounds of the preparations going on all around her, and the smell of the chlorine spelled home to Kate. The packed bleachers looked like a faceless sea of people, yet she felt like she knew each one of the spectators. Even the extra seating in the upper deck behind the glass windows overflowed.

Snapping out of her daze, Kate glanced up and down a few rows of bleachers, looking for her mom, but gave up her search and hurried to the starting block to squeeze in a warm-up. She spit into her goggles to prevent them from fogging and then pulled them over her eyes. She swam a few brisk laps in the Olympic-sized pool and gave herself a pep talk.

You can do this.

This is no different than any other meet.

This is swimming. It's what you do better than anyone here.

You're most at home in the pool.

Just swim like you've been swimming.

You can do this, Kate.

This is no different than. . .

The whistle blew its warning, and the swimmers cleared the pool. Kate toweled off and stood with her team during the National Anthem. She put her right hand over her heart, but she hopped and moved around on her feet to keep her muscles warm and shook her left arm to keep it limber. The instant the last bars faded, the sounds of the crowd, the water, and the swimmers erupted into an instant roar. She shook her right arm out and readjusted her goggles on her forehead. *It's time.*

By some miracle, she happened to look to the right, straight at her mom. Mom sat beside an empty space—the only one in the whole place, Kate thought. She imagined her dad sitting there, holding his wife's hand, cheering for his daughter.

Kate begged her mom for encouragement

with her eyes. She smiled, nodded, and then put her hands together in a symbol of promised prayer. Kate squeezed her eyes shut for a brief moment and nodded her thanks as she climbed onto the block.

"Swimmers, take your mark. . . ." Kate closed her eyes. *Lord, help me.* When the gun blasted its call to action, she sprang off the block. She sailed through the water with the ease of a dolphin. Kate pictured her mom watching with tears in her eyes. By the turn on her last of four laps, Kate glanced to the sides and saw no disturbance to the water on either side of her—not even one swimmer competed for the win.

Reinvigorated by the taste of impending victory, Kate pulled from deep within her and gathered everything she had to finish the last length of the race. Fifteen meters, ten meters, final pull, glide, touch. The race ended as quickly as it started. She, a first-year swimmer, had just won her first race at State. *Could it be enough for a new record?* Kate lifted her head and peeled off her goggles to check her time.

As soon as the water cleared her ears, she heard the riotous cheers. One by one, the other swimmers glided into the timer pad. She had won the race with a huge margin—but no new record.

Over the PA system, Kate heard, "Kate Walker has taken first place in the 200–meter free."

She floated on her back for a moment, allowing her body to cool down. *I won!* She couldn't let her victory become clouded with disappointment over not setting the record. *I won!*

Cooled down, she hoisted herself onto the pool deck, and Coach Thompson ran to hug her.

"Congratulations, hon. You deserve this."

"Congratulations, Kate." People she didn't know were shaking her hand.

"Congrats, girlfriend." Pam patted her on the back as she walked by.

Kate stumbled toward the locker room, still in a fog, unable to really wrap her mind around what had happened. *I did it,* Kate said to herself. *I did it.* She looked up to the stands where she had found her mom before the race and saw her wipe away the tears. She gave Kate a big thumbs-up and nodded her head, grinning from ear to ear.

With at least an hour before her next race, Kate rummaged through her bag for a protein bar and a big bottle of water and headed for the locker room. The cheers and congratulations rang in her ears. *Come on, hold it together—just one more minute.*

Once inside the locker room, she ran to a bathroom stall. As soon as the door swung shut, she pressed her forehead against the cool metal door and collapsed into sobs. She couldn't hold it back any longer. She watched as the tears ran down and dripped onto the floor. She took a raggedy breath and sat back, rubbing her eyes. *Too much pent-up emotion.*

About forty-five minutes later, Kate's team took third place in the IM relay and second place in the free relay. Coach had told Kate not to push too hard. She really wanted her to save as much energy as possible for her last and most important—hopefully, record-setting—race.

Kate needed a break. In ninety minutes, she'd be swimming her last race. She moved around the pool deck and gave herself little pep talks the whole time, trying to keep her mind focused and her muscles warm. *Yawn.* She stretched and hopped side to side. *Come on, wake up.*

"Hey, Kate." Coach came up behind her. "You seem to be fading. Why don't you go eat a granola bar or a banana?" She put her hands on each side of Kate's face and looked into her eyes. "You really need to perk up, kiddo. It's crunch time. This is the most important race of the year. I didn't want to tell you this, but do you see that lady over there?" Coach pointed to a pretty woman in a sage green dress on the sidelines with a clipboard in her lap. When Kate nodded, she continued, "She's the head coach of the OSU team. She asked about you."

Kate was stunned. "She did? What did she say?"

"She asked me to keep you going and to point you in her direction when it got to be picking time. She said that she imagined she'd have a full ride for you if you keep it up."

"Oh, wow! Talk about pressure! I'm so glad you told me, though. It really gives me something to swim for right now." She yawned again. Why was she so tired?

Coach eyed her. "Kate, I'm not kidding. You need to go get some fuel in your body. But it's getting close, so don't eat too much." She put her hands on Kate's shoulders and steered her toward the locker room.

Pam and Brittany followed her in. "Hey, we heard what Coach said. That's so cool!" Pam patted her on the back.

Kate collapsed onto the bench in front of her locker. "Yeah, it sure is, but I'm so nervous. I'm just not feeling it. What if I bomb?" Her knuckles were white as she squeezed the seat beside her legs.

"You'll be fine, Kate. You can do this in your sleep." Brittany waved her hand in the air. "No problem."

What am I going to do? I can't do this without help—but I promised Mom. Kate shook her head to clear her doubts. She made a quick decision. "You guys, I need a Red Dragon. Please tell me you have an extra." Kate looked up at them with puppy eyes.

"Oh man, I was worried you were going to say that. We each just drank one, and I gave one to Sandy. We don't have any more. I'm really sorry." Pam knitted her eyebrows, looking concerned.

"Oh no. And there's no time to go out for one. Do you know anyone else who might have some?"

They both shook their heads with regret. "Not anyone who's here."

Kate plopped on the bench in despair. "Okay, I'm going to have to put any hopes of an energy supplement out of my mind and find my energy from within, right?" She peeled a banana and took a bite. She practically swallowed without chewing and then threw half of it away. She paced the floor. "There's nothing left for me to do."

"Not necessarily, Kate." Pam and Brittany eyed each other, and Kate saw Brittany shake her head. Pam nodded and opened her locker.

"Kate, I just need you to trust me. Take one of these." She held out the palm of her hand. In it lay a tiny blue pill.

Speed. With wide eyes and an open mouth, she looked from the pill to Pam and then over to Brittany and back to the pill. She could tell by the way they were acting that Pam held the real thing.

"Pam. . .I. . .um. . .I. . .don't know what to say." Kate stalled, trying to think. "Where on earth did you get that?"

"Now, Kate. We're in the big leagues. Everyone takes these. It's pretty much expected." She talked fast while Brittany just nodded. "In fact, when you walked off to the locker room, Coach motioned for us to follow you because she knows, without being able to come right out and say it, that this is what you need right now. I promise you, you'll sail through this race. You'll thank me for this."

Kate shook her head. No way Coach Thompson was involved. But she couldn't worry about that right now—no time. "My mom would kill me if she knew I even considered it.

And I'd probably be yanked off the team for
even thinking about it, let alone actually doing
it. What are you guys thinking? No way." Kate
swung her head side to side the whole time she
talked—*Olivia, why couldn't it be you standing
here with me right now?*

"Don't get all preachy and whiny on me.
You've got to get a backbone and do what it
takes to get through this race with a bang. It's
not the time to be a prissy mama's girl."

Someone came in to use the bathroom,
so Pam lowered her voice to a whisper. "Kate,
you're running out of time. This is it. You have
no more time to prepare yourself. Are you ready
to get on the block and swim in the state you're
in right now?"

Kate shook her head and looked down,
twisting her swim cap in her fists.

"I didn't think so," Pam rushed, almost out
of time. "Look, I can promise you that your
mom would never tell you to take this little
pill, but I can also promise you that her trust
on an issue as minor as this"—she held out the
pill again—"is far less important than a college
scholarship. You *will not* get caught, and you
will swim the race of your life. Kate, there's
really no decision here."

IT'S DECISION TIME!

The time has come for Kate to make a very difficult decision. Think long and hard about what you would do if you encountered the exact same circumstances that Kate is facing. It's easy to say that you'd make the right choice. But are you sure that you could say no and risk a college scholarship? What if your mom struggled with only one income and didn't have the money to send you to college? What if you truly believed you wouldn't get caught and promised yourself that you'd never ever take another drug or energy supplement again? Would you consider doing it? Would you be tempted? Are you sure?

Once you make your decision, turn to the corresponding page to see how it turns out for Kate—and for you.

Turn to page 124 if Kate is able to stay strong and refuses to take the drug.

Turn to page 159 if Kate decides to take the pill— just this once.

❀

The next three chapters tell the story of what happened to Kate when she decided to do what she knew was right.

Chapter 10

DIFFERENT STROKES

The clock ticked on the locker room wall while Kate stared at the little blue pill in Pam's hand. Her thoughts spilled over each other; and every time she opened her mouth, the words just stuck to her dry tongue. Finally, she looked at Pam and then at Brittany. "I'm not taking speed," she sputtered. "I can't believe you even thought I might." She shook her head. "We'll talk about this after I swim. I have to go now."

"Well. . .I. . .I mean. . ." Pam's face reddened like she'd been slapped.

Kate spun on her heels and bustled out of the locker room. She held her head up high and her shoulders back, confident she'd done the right thing. But right or not, she still had to find a way to swim her race, even though she wanted to just collapse on a bench. A new level of nervousness assailed her senses—one she never imagined.

For once, Kate couldn't hear the sounds on the pool deck because of the drone in her ears. She couldn't smell her beloved chlorine because her chest ached and she couldn't take a deep breath. And now, facing her most important swim ever, she'd thrown it all away—any chance at a record and a college scholarship—by not preparing mentally and physically.

Kate squared her shoulders, took a deep breath, and set off to find a secluded corner of the deck to collect herself in the minutes before the race. She passed a few people who called out her name but ignored them. She'd given too much time to external things. Right now she needed to focus within herself, to take a moment to pray.

After a few jumping jacks, Kate shook her arms, trying to loosen them up. She rotated her head from side to side in half circles, and stared at her hands, willing them to stop shaking.

"You okay?" Coach approached her with concern in her eyes.

"I don't know, Coach." She shook her head

and looked down at her still-shaking hands. "I can't focus. I'm not ready to get in the water. I wish I had another hour."

"Well, kiddo, you don't." Coach put her hands on each of Kate's shoulders and made solid contact with her stormy sea-green eyes. "Whatever it is, Kate, whatever happened. . ."

Kate opened her mouth to speak.

"No, don't tell me, we don't have time to let your mind go there now. Whatever went on in that locker room, it just doesn't matter."

"But. . . ," Kate protested.

"Listen to me." Coach squeezed her shoulders a little bit tighter.

Kate looked away, but Coach moved into her line of vision, forcing her to maintain eye contact. "Even if it matters more than anything, nothing can change it over the next few minutes. Five minutes from this very second, you'll be done swimming; and you can think about whatever it is that's troubling you for as long as you want to think about it."

She tightened her grip on Kate's shoulders. "Right now, though, you need to focus. You'll regret it if you don't take control of yourself, Kate. Look at me. You can do this. You know how to swim this race instinctively better

than any swimmer I've ever had the pleasure
of coaching. You have a very long future in
swimming still ahead of you."

Kate shook her head, hopeless. "But what
if. . . ?"

Coach brushed her off. "Your swimming
future—no matter how much you've told
yourself it does—does not ride on this one
swim. Take some pressure off yourself. Lighten
your load, and get out there and do what you
love to do. Let the water wash away your cares.
Listen to the sounds of the rushing water, not
the voices in your head. Shut them off." Coach
waited, searching her eyes. "Are you doing it?"

She gave a weak nod.

"Come on, kiddo." Coach released her grip.
"You. Can. Do. It. Do it. Do it." She whispered,
pounding her fists in the air in front of Kate's face.

Kate offered her coach a shaky smile, second
by second taking more control of herself. She
looked from her coach to the pool and then
back to her coach and nodded. "I'm good."

Satisfied, Coach didn't say another word and
steered Kate toward the starting blocks.

"Swimmers take your mark. . . . Get set. . . ."

The gun went off, and Kate flew off the
block. Awesome start, maybe her best ever! She

swam with all of her might and talked to herself the whole way. *Come on, Kate. You can do it, Kate. Don't think about it, Kate. Don't. . .*

But no matter how hard she tried to prevent it, her mind wandered back to the little pill. She couldn't believe that she'd allowed herself to come so close to taking drugs. How had that happened? She pictured a bent radar antenna coming from her brain. Apparently, she'd been clouded and blinded by the glamour of being the best. So clouded that she almost risked everything for success.

Having trouble clearing her mind, Kate forgot to watch the lanes next to her as each stroke brought faces to her mind: Mom, Julia, Olivia, Pastor Rick, Mark, Olivia, Mom, Dad. . . . *Oh, Dad, did you see me today? Did I scare you? I'm so sorry, Dad.*

What is that scripture? There's no temptation that I might face that isn't common to everyone? Something like that. Okay, I was tempted. I passed the test. Right? Right. Now swim, Kate. Swim! Kate snapped back to attention as she realized that she only had about half a pool length to swim in her first State competition. She glanced to the right. Clear. To the left—a swimmer almost neck and neck with her! Panic set in—

she could still win it, or she could give up. Kate knew what she had to do.

She tucked her head down, reached a little farther, and pulled a little harder. She turned to breathe every fifth stroke instead of every third—her lungs on fire.

Fifteen meters—

Ten meters—

PULL!

Five meters—

Stretch!

She gave it all she had and touched the timer pad with the very tips of her fingers before she slammed the full force of her body into it. The swimmer beside her plowed into her timer mere milliseconds later. But that was all Kate needed to place first.

Kate pulled off her goggles and patted her closest competitor on the back. "Nice swim."

But she didn't have to look at the timer to know she hadn't set a record. She'd swum a good race, some would say great, but not a record-breaking swim. It didn't matter, though. She had won a different kind of race today— one that she knew would impact her life in even bigger ways. Definitely cause for celebration.

She climbed out of the pool, breathless and

shaky. The team ran over to her and jumped up and down, suffocating her with hugs. *Smile, Kate.* Their hands slapped on her wet back, and her hand got pumped by numerous, faceless people. She couldn't see out of the crowd that encircled her, so she had no idea if Pam and Brittany stood among the cheering crowd. But it didn't matter. This was her moment—no one could take it away from her.

After the fervor died down, Kate looked up to the bleachers where her mom still sat. Kate held up one open hand, asking for five minutes. Mom nodded and beamed at her, clearly proud, and reached into her purse. Kate smiled when her mom pulled out a tissue to wipe tears from her eyes.

In the locker room, Kate looked up and down the aisles hoping to find Pam and Brittany so they could talk. She heard the zip of duffle bags, the flushing of toilets, someone with headphones on sang off-key—but no Pam and no Brittany. Kate sighed. She really didn't want to have this conversation by phone. It would probably have to wait until school on Monday. Oh well, she'd have some time to think things through and work out what she wanted to say to them.

"So, what's going on, Kate?" Mom didn't waste a single second when the car finally turned on to the expressway and they started on their trip home through the mountain pass. "You should be much happier, but you seem so solemn. What happened? Did your coach get mad at you for not breaking the record?" Mom's eyes flared like a struck match at the possibility.

"Oh no! Not at all, Mom. In fact, before the race she even told me to take some pressure off and to just do it because I love it."

"Oh, okay then." Mom sighed in relief. "I don't want you put under a lot of pressure. . . . So. . ."

"There is something wrong." Kate hesitated. "I'll tell you all about it. I need to." She spilled the whole story out onto the dashboard. At least she didn't have to start from the very beginning—Mom already knew that part. "You were right. It was leading down a dangerous road, one I almost traveled."

"Yes." Mom squeezed her eyes shut for a brief moment, and her lips moved as if in prayer. "I'm so relieved that you see that. So, what now?"

"I don't know, Mom. I just don't know."

"Well, let me ask it this way, then." She bit her lip. "What is it about all that's happened exactly, that's upsetting you the most?"

"I guess I'm upset that Pam and Brittany are doing drugs." She contemplated her answer for a moment and then added, "And I'm upset they offered them to me."

"Is that all?"

"Yeah. I. . .um. . .I think so. I'm not sure. I just feel unsettled," Kate said, feeling confused but still not sure why. "That's why I didn't want to ride back with the team."

"Do you want to know what I think, sweetie?" When Kate nodded, she continued. "I think those are two of the reasons, but I don't think they're the main ones."

Kate scrunched the corners of her eyes and peered through her lashes at her mom, perplexed. "What do you mean? What other reasons would I have?"

"I think more than anything, you're mad at yourself. I think you realize you were spiritually unaware of the danger you were in. You risked some big trouble over some issues you've always prided yourself on being able to avoid. You found yourself right in the middle of temptation, and it scares you. I think you're also mad at yourself because you came close to doing it. Thank God you didn't"—Mom blinked her eyes, moisture coating her lashes—"but you came close, didn't you?" She spoke in a casual tone, but white knuckles gripped the steering wheel.

"Well. . .I wouldn't exactly say 'close.' But I definitely considered it. I felt the weight of all that was riding on my performance, and I thought maybe I could do it just once and never again."

"There would have always been a next time, Kate. Once you take one step, it's far too easy to take the next step because there are fewer unknowns with the second step and even fewer inhibitions with the third and the fourth. It's a slippery slope."

Kate nodded. Looked like Mom had been right. "Yeah, that makes sense. I am mad at myself, I guess. I mean, how could I have let that happen? Even worse, how did I not see it coming? What if I had taken that pill?"

"Whoa, one question at a time." Mom laughed. "How could you let that happen? Because you're human, Kate. You didn't want to see that your dependency was misplaced on energy sources other than the true Lifegiver. But thankfully, God doesn't expect you to be perfect. He just expects you to get back on the right path when you realize you've veered off it."

Kate flipped the zipper of her duffel bag back and forth while she listened.

"How did you not see it coming? Because you wanted to be a part of the elite group. You wanted to be in control of your body and make it do what you wanted to do. You didn't want to see that what you were doing was wrong." She loosened her grip on the steering wheel and shook out her right hand. "As to your last question, what if you had taken that pill? I'll tell you, Kate, it could have been bad. If you guys had been caught somehow, you'd have had trouble with the police. Or worse, you could have had some kind of physical reaction to it and had trouble in the pool. But even if none of that happened, it would have continued. That wouldn't have been the end of the drugs."

"No, probably not." Kate looked out the window at her beloved mountains zooming by. "What now?"

"I think you need to pray about what to do, sweetie. You're going to have to figure this one out for yourself. In the end, though, Pam's and

Brittany's parents are going to have to know. You realize that, right?"

"Yeah, I guess. I'm not quite sure how to deal with that, though."

"I could tell you what to do. But I'm not going to this time." Mom shook her head. "You need to think about things and pray for a solution. I'll support whatever you come up with."

Lord, help me know what to do now.

Sunday morning dawned bright. Sunshine shed hope and clarity on the previous night's darkness. Before leaving for church, Kate decided to call Pam—she had to get it over with. "I hate to say this on the phone, Pam, because I'm afraid you won't understand my intent from the tone of my voice. I'm not angry; I'm scared. I don't want you to hate me, but I have to take that chance. I can't go on and pretend I don't know what's going on. What if something happened to you or to Brittany, or whoever else is involved, and I had done nothing to stop it? I could never live with myself."

Pam's silence was deafening.

"So. . ." Kate could feel her nerve stuttering

and weakening, threatening to abandon her completely, but she pressed on. "I. . .I have no choice but to bring it all into the light. I'll give you guys until school starts tomorrow to talk to Coach Thompson or to your parents. But someone's going to have to know what's going on."

"You wouldn't." Pam's shaky voice belied her bravado.

Kate bit her fingernail too low. Everyone would hate her. "I—I—I have to, Pam. I wish this wasn't even going on, but I can't pretend. Not only is it wrong, it's dangerous." Kate had to fight to keep from whining. She didn't have to convince Pam of the right thing. She just had to do it.

"Wrong? Who are you to decide what's wrong? We are held to such high standards as swimmers that we can't possibly live up to them without help of some kind. Wrong? What's 'wrong' anyway?" She snorted in disgust.

Kate sat down on a stool, choosing her next words very carefully. "Pam, God decides what's wrong. He tells us to follow the law and to honor our parents. It's wrong to take drugs because it's illegal, dangerous, and disobedient."

"Oh, you're kidding me? You're one of *those*?" She snorted. "I had no idea you were a religious nut."

"I told you a bunch of times that I went to church, Pam. It's not like it was a secret."

"A lot of people go to church, Kate. I even go to church. But that doesn't mean anything. So what? You go to church. But how does that make you the judge and jury?"

Anger spewed from Pam's mouth, and Kate didn't blame her—she probably felt betrayed. Shame washed over Kate. How could she have spent so much time with these girls but never shared her faith? "Well, I'm sorry. I guess I didn't let you see that part of me well enough. I'm really sorry about that. But the facts are the facts." This wasn't going anywhere—no point in arguing more. "Look, I'm going to let you go. We're leaving for church now. Think about what I said. I'm not backing down from it."

On the drive to church, one of Pastor Rick's famous lines kept running through her mind. "Going to church doesn't make you a Christian any more than going to McDonalds makes you a hamburger."

Chapter 11

DE-CELEBRATIONS

Hesitantly peering around the door frame to the office, Kate whispered, "Coach, do you have a few minutes?"

"Kate, come on in! I'm so glad to see you. . . but why aren't you at lunch?" She slid her desk chair back and gestured toward the guest chair.

"I'm really not hungry. I wanted to talk to you."

"Okay, well, have a seat. First, how is your day going? You're a big celebrity around here!" Coach grinned.

"Oh, it's great, Coach." Kate tried to sound as excited as she knew Coach wanted her to be. It had been a victory for them both, and Kate knew she owed it to her to let her enjoy the moment. "Everyone is so excited and supportive. I can't wait until next season."

"You're going to be swimming with the boys' team practices, right? They start next week." Coach peered over her glasses. "You need to keep your skills up in the off-season."

"Oh, definitely. I just meant that I couldn't wait for next year's competition. I'll be in the pool every day until then. It'll be fun to swim with the boys' team, too. I'll get to see how their workouts are different than ours. . ." Her voice trailed off as she picked at a loose thread on her jeans.

"Okay, kiddo, what's going on?" Coach got serious. "I assume this is about whatever was bothering you before your last race."

Kate nodded, unable to speak through her quivering lips and pounding heart.

"Did someone give you a hard time?" Coach leaned forward, eyes intent.

"N–n–no. It isn't that. Not really." She took a deep breath. "Something happened, Coach. Something's been happening, actually." She launched into the whole story. Told Coach about the energy supplements and the caffeine pills. Explained about how Mom found her stash and made her stop and how pulling back from all those things had affected her swimming for a few days.

Coach nodded. "Ahh. That explains it."

While she finished the story, Coach looked down at her desk, clicking her pen open and closed, open and closed, open and closed.

"Then, at State. . .well. . . ," Kate stammered, not wanting to continue. Her friends would hate her.

"It's okay. Whatever it is, you can tell me." Coach put down her pen and gave Kate her full attention.

"They offered me speed. The real thing."

Coach Thompson peered at Kate over her glasses with her mouth wide open.

The ticking of the clock on the wall filled the room like a ticking time bomb.

"Are you sure, Kate?"

Kate nodded. "Not only that, but Pam said that it was partly your idea. . .that you wanted her to offer the pill to me so I'd swim better." She hung her head, knowing that last part would hurt.

"Wow. I can't think of anything that would have surprised me more. I thought I knew this team better than that." She rubbed her temples and squeezed her eyes shut. "I mean, I knew you guys fooled around with those goofy energy drinks. But even though I didn't really like it, I thought they were harmless."

Kate gave her a minute to process all she'd just heard and then continued. "I told Pam that I would give her and Brittany until school started today to come forward on their own. They chose not to, so I had to do it. I'm sure they thought I was just bluffing. But this is too important to just ignore."

When Kate ran out of words, she just sat there, silent. The bell for her next class rang—she wouldn't be going. She gazed sympathetically at the coach she'd come to love, sure that Coach had no idea what to do next. What could she do to help?

"Kate, it's times like these that I wonder if I'm in the right profession. I guess I would have thought that I was doing a good enough job of making everyone feel valued for who they are and not for what I wanted out of them. No one on this team should ever feel so much pressure that they become capable of something like this." She shook her head and rubbed her forehead so hard it turned red.

"Coach, I don't see it that way. We all create our own pressure. You actually detract from it by talking us down and telling us to have fun. Any pressure we feel is our own doing."

Knock, knock. Both of them jumped. Coach

opened the office door then stuck her head out into the hallway. "Come on in. I think I know why you're here." She sat back down in her seat and waited for Pam, Brittany, and Sandy to squeeze past her into the tiny office.

Pam glared at Kate, who occupied the only other chair in the room, and slumped onto the floor in defeat. Brittany and Sandy didn't look at her as they took a place on the floor beside Pam.

Looking from one girl to the next Coach said, "I am so disappointed, girls." She shook her head from side to side, over and over. Finally, she put both hands on her thighs and heaved her small body out of the chair as though a weight pressed down on her. "I'm going to have to bring your parents and Principal Coleman into this. So, why don't you hang on before you say anything? I'll give you each a chance to speak, but let's save it until the principal gets down here. I'll be just outside the door using the phone." Coach left them alone.

Squirming, Kate looked at everything in the room but the other girls.

"Why couldn't you just leave it alone, Kate?" Sandy broke the silence. "We wouldn't have pushed you. You could have kept doing your thing, and we'd have left you alone. Why?"

Kate shook her head, her lip trembling again.

"I mean, do you realize that we'll all be off the team?" Sandy's voice was laced with venom. "You crippled the team by what you did, Kate. How can you live with that?"

Kate had enough. She sat up straight and slammed her fists on her armrests. "How can I live with that? *Me?* I crippled this team? *Me?* Sandy, you guys made the choices you did, and you involved me in them." Kate looked down at her hands. "I'll admit to my own weaknesses and that I used substances as a crutch, too. But it crossed the line for me when it became illegal. I can't go that far. I have to do what's right. I have no choice."

"When did you get all high and mighty, anyway? It's not like you've been a goody-goody this whole time." Sandy put her head back against the wall.

"You know,"—Kate looked at each of the girls—"that's my one big regret in all of this. I am so sorry that I hid my faith from you guys. It wasn't a conscious choice. I don't even know why it happened like that, actually. I should have let you guys in to that part of my life. Who knows, maybe you'd have made a different choice about offering me drugs, or even taking them yourselves, if you'd seen Christ in me. But whether you believe me or not, my faith is a very important part of my life."

Pam snorted in disgust—the first sound Kate had heard from her in over twenty-four hours.

"Pam, I know you feel the most betrayed, and you don't believe I'm a Christian like I say I am. That's okay. I have to live with that. I've learned a lot about why it's very important to make people aware of where my priorities are."

"That still doesn't tell me why you couldn't just walk away and leave it alone, Kate. Maybe you just want us off the team so you don't have to compete against us." Sandy crossed her arms and glared.

Her snide remark twisted in Kate's gut. "It's not that at all, Sandy. What you said doesn't even make sense. This whole thing was a big mess and. . .well. . .I had to try to fix it." She shrugged her shoulders. "Plus, it was the only way to get you guys to stop using drugs. Think about it. Not only did you risk yourself every time you got into the pool on drugs, but you were also risking our team."

All three girls rolled their eyes, but Kate continued, undaunted. "If you had gotten caught, it would have been made public and the whole team would have been under scrutiny, not to mention our titles, wins, records, and even Coach and the school would have been called into question."

Kate shook her head. "But that's not even the most important thing, which is you guys. I couldn't sit by and watch this happen right in front of me and do nothing." She opened her mouth and took a breath, not quite finished but unsure of how to go on. "What if we had to scrape one of you off the pool bottom one day after you had a heart attack because your heart rate got too high? How would I have felt knowing I could have prevented it?" She shuddered at the thought.

"And. . .well, I feel like I've done a disservice to my faith by not being a Christian example to you guys. I want to be that now, even if it means some of you get hurt for the short term. I wish it had unfolded differently, but that's the way it is now." Finished, Kate hung her head in the silent room. She wished someone would speak, but the silence remained unbroken until Coach Thompson and Principal Coleman walked into the room carrying an extra chair.

The principal sat in the chair and crossed

her legs, her high-heeled shoe falling to
the floor. "Okay, who wants to start? What
happened?"

After a long silence, Kate opened her mouth
to speak.

Principal Coleman shook her head and held
up her finger. "I think I'd like to hear the story
from one of the others."

Chapter 12

TRUE FRIENDSHIP

Oh, Olivia. Why haven't I been a better friend?

With Christmas break drawing to a close, Kate feared that she'd let too much time pass and there would be no way to fix things with Olivia. But she couldn't put it off any longer. Kate took a deep breath, pressed the speed-dial button, and closed her bedroom door. She walked to the corner of the room, pressed her back into the wall, and slid to the floor. When she heard Olivia's voice, she started the conversation with the plaintive plea of a kitten. "Can you ever forgive me?"

Olivia answered with a clipped and aloof tone. "Forgive you for what? I'm kind of busy. Can we talk another time?"

Ouch. Kate deserved that. "Liv, I screwed up. I know I've been a selfish, terrible friend. I hope you can forgive me and let me make it up to you." Her voice caught. "Don't shut me out. . ."

"You're the one who shut me out, Kate," Olivia reminded her. "You have no need for me anymore. I'm of no use to you." She had never heard Olivia sound so sad.

"No, Liv, that's where you're wrong. I have no explanation; I'm not even going to try to convince you. I'm hoping we can just start over, though. If you can forgive me and we just erase the past few weeks, we'll be back to normal."

Silence.

"What do you say, Liv? Please?"

"Well, I don't know. . . ," she teased, sounding like her old self.

Kate's shoulders relaxed, and she breathed a deep sigh of relief. She could tell that Olivia's heart had softened. She'd never let life get in the way of making time for her best friend ever again.

The doorbell rang at the same instant as she hung up the phone.

Mark! Kate scurried to change her clothes. She couldn't believe she'd forgotten their plans to go for a walk in the snow. Hurrying down the stairs, she pulled on her mittens and then went into the night.

They walked in silence under the stars as the snow fell.

How can I say this? Kate knew she needed to be honest. "This vacation has been an incredible two weeks. We've had so much time to spend together, and I've enjoyed every single second of it." She bit her lip.

"But?" he prodded.

"But I'm afraid that by rushing into a relationship that I'm not ready for, it will be the death of a wonderful friendship. . . . I don't want to risk our friendship, Mark."

"I know what you mean." He looked up into the sky and let the snowflakes hit his wind-burned cheeks. "It just sort of felt like this was supposed to be our next step, and I didn't want to let the opportunity get away from us. Because you're important to me—you always have been."

Kate nodded and blew steam from her mouth. "You know what?"

"No, what?" Mark answered and laughed, tweaking her on the chin.

"If we're really meant to be more than friends, a couple of years wouldn't make a difference, right?"

"No, I suppose it wouldn't."

"But if we're not meant to have that kind of relationship, then by rushing into it, it will cost us a great friendship."

"Hmm, that's a great way to look at it." He slipped a casual arm around her shoulders as they walked.

"So, let's just step back to what we know we can handle and put the rest on hold. I mean, we'll still be together all the time, so nothing will change. We have band practice and our gigs, plus we can hang out anytime without the pressure of a relationship."

"I'm all for that, Kate." He actually looked relieved. "Will you promise me one thing, though?" He had a twinkle in his eye.

"Sure, what?"

"Don't let anyone else have your first kiss. Okay? It's all mine." He winked and gave her a gorgeous grin.

Her stomach flipped. Friends could still be handsome, right?

"Deal!" They shook hands and laughed.

How could Christmas break be over already? Kate couldn't believe how fast it had gone.

She groaned, rolled over, and pulled the covers over her head. Her body clock still beat to the rhythm of vacation.

When she finally pulled herself from her bed, she had to rush to get out of the house for her first swim practice with the boys' team. It would be strange without Pam and Sandy to swim with—they were the only other ones swimming off-season. So she'd be the only girl in the pool with twenty boys.

Ugh! The boys might not like having me there. I'm a nark, after all. Kate's thoughts ran wild as she hurried to get out of the house. The drive to the school ended way too fast.

"Hi, Kate," the boys' team called out in one voice when Coach Thompson introduced her.

"She'll be the only one from the girls' team joining us for now. I hope you'll all make her feel welcome." Coach narrowed her focus to include each boy. "This is your season. Kate won't get in the way of your practices. She's just here to swim and stay in shape."

"Well, that shouldn't be hard for her."

Kate turned beet red but had no idea which boy said that. Several others snickered.

"Okay, let's not be childish, boys," Coach scolded. "Come on now, go swim." She sent

them off to find their lane assignments and
workout schedule.

"Hey, Kate."

She turned from the bleachers to find two
popular seniors waiting to say something to her.

"Yeah?" She braced herself.

The tallest one said, "We just wanted you
to know that we're glad you turned in the girls
for using speed. Junk like that gives sports a bad
name." He looked shy. "So. . .good for you."

He left before she had a chance to thank
him. Smiling, she eased herself into the cold
water and adjusted her goggles. *Ahhh. Home.*
She started her swim at a steady pace, warming
up her muscles that had been on a two-week
hiatus. She eased her speed up to a clip that
would tax her, but not force her to crawl from
the pool in agony.

How could water be so healing? She let its
purity wash away all of her worries and cares.
It cleansed her soul and comforted her heart.
Nothing mattered in the pool.

Sitting at a desk, Kate looked out the window,
lost in her thoughts of walking with Mark the
night before. She chewed the end of her pencil,

152

knowing she'd done the right thing.

"Hey, Kate."

She dropped her pencil as a voice at her left shoulder snapped her back from her snowy memories. *Sandy.*

"Hey." Kate looked down.

"We don't have much time before class. But I wanted to tell you that I did a lot of thinking over the holiday." The bell cut her off. "I'll have to talk to you later, okay?" She left before Kate could respond.

A little later, after the third-period bell rang, Kate and Mark walked into the bustling lunchroom. As always, students climbed over benches, bags were tossed from one table to the next, and smells had mingled into an unidentifiable biohazard. While they waited in line, she took a quick look around and immediately noticed Pam and Brittany on one of the benches right outside the commons. They saw Kate and looked the other way, whispering. Kate sighed, hopes of forgiveness and the restoration of their friendships. . .impossible.

"Hey, what did you expect?" Mark read her mind as they slid onto a seat with one of the red plastic lunch trays that always smelled of mildew. "They weren't really your friends, anyway. They didn't even know the real you."

"I know." She poked at her food. "I just hoped they'd have figured some things out in the time away."

"Just pray for them. Keep praying for them. Someone outside of the situation will have to show them what's what before they're ever going to be able to come around and forgive you."

"That's probably very true." She played with her food. "I'll have to just pray that the Lord sends someone their way who can help them see the truth."

"Kate, can I talk to you for a minute?" Sandy asked in a soft voice near Kate's shoulder.

Kate coughed, choking on her drink.

"Hi, Sandy. Sure you can. Have a seat." Mark grabbed his apple off the tray and waved good-bye as he headed to his class while Sandy sat in his spot.

Kate looked at the clock. "We've only got about ten minutes."

"Probably. If I were you, I wouldn't even want to listen that long." She took a deep breath and looked into Kate's eyes. "I'm really sorry. You were so right about everything and. . .well. . .I have a secret to tell you."

Kate leaned forward.

"Well, I take that back; it's not going to be a secret anymore. It's something I've kept separate from school but shouldn't have." She took another deep breath and looked down at the table. "I'm a Christian, too. There, I said it." She exhaled and looked Kate in the eye. "Why is it so hard for me to tell people? It shouldn't be, but it just is."

Kate smiled. "Sandy, I'm so glad you told me. You're right, it shouldn't be. But I understand. It's like Peter. . ." Kate shared with Sandy the same story that Mark had reminded her of a few weeks ago. "So, you see, even Peter failed when it came time to share his faith in Jesus. None of us are perfect, but the question is how are you going to change now that you know? No more secrets, right?"

Sandy nodded then lowered her big brown eyes. "I'm afraid, though."

"Sure you are. It's okay to be afraid. It's only not okay if you let it cripple you into doing nothing." Kate looked up and rubbed her chin. "Hey, I've been thinking about starting something, and I think that now might be the perfect time."

Sandy eyes lit up, and she took a bite of Kate's uneaten brownie.

Kate waved her hand, offering her the whole thing. "I think we should start a Bible study group before school. I know Mark would join and a few others. We could take turns leading the group. It would only be for about twenty minutes right before class. What do you think?"

Sandy's big eyes grew even larger. "Oh, wow. Talk about making waves." She took a deep breath. "Well, it's time for me to put up or shut up, I guess. Count me in." Sandy smiled and ate the rest of Kate's brownie.

Exactly two weeks later, Kate rushed to get dressed after her early morning swim so she could get to the first Bible study meeting on time. She jogged down the long hall from the locker room to the meeting room that Principal Coleman offered for their use. Rushing in the door, almost late, she joined the eleven students who had arranged their seats in a large oval. Several even had Bibles with them. Panting to catch her breath, Kate slid in between Mark and Sandy and tucked her bag under her seat.

"Welcome to the first meeting of our new Bible study and prayer group." Mark smiled warmly. "First, I want you to know I've been so excited ever since Kate came to me with her idea about starting this group. That there are students in this school who will give up their time and risk having a reputation of being a religious fanatic"—several students giggled at the term— "because of their passion for Christ . . .well. . .I'm at a loss for words. It sure lit a fire in me."

He nodded as he looked around the room. "This group right here,"—Mark spread his arms out to include all the students—"this is our core group. We are called by God to be leaders in this school, to share the gospel, and to be examples of Christ." He looked right at several of them. "You want to know how I know He's called you for that?"

They all nodded, transfixed.

"Two reasons. One, because He's called me, too. We're all called to be ambassadors for the cause of Christ—every single one of us. And two, because you're willing—you're here. That's it. That's all it takes to be used by God."

Mark opened up his Bible. "This is what I want for us to be to each other here in this group. . .it's the same thing that Paul asked of his friends as recorded in Ephesians, chapter six. Paul asked them to 'Pray also for me, that whenever I open my mouth, words may be given me so that I will fearlessly make known the mystery of the gospel, for which I am an ambassador in chains. Pray that I may declare it fearlessly, as I should.'"

Kate stared at Mark, humbled by his words and impressed by his clear thoughts. He'd make a great preacher one day.

Mark closed his Bible and looked around the circle. "So, let's commit to each other to be here each week. We'll have a prayer time, a short devotion which we can take turns leading, and then time to share concerns." He smiled at the group. "Eventually, people will want what we have, and this room will be overflowing."

At just that precise moment, the door slowly creaked open. Kate and Sandy stared with open mouths as Pam and Brittany peeked into the room. After a brief hesitation, Pam timidly asked, "Is it too late to join you guys?"

Kate smiled and scooted her chair over to make room in the circle. "It's never too late."

The next three chapters tell the story of what happened to Kate when she chose to take the pill Pam offered her.

Chapter 10

NO ONE WILL KNOW

Before she could change her mind, Kate grabbed the little pill out of Pam's hand and gulped it down without water. Starving for confidence and desperate for success, it seemed her only option. She waited. No fireworks went off inside her—just yet. After about five minutes, she felt the warmth traveling through her body. It started with her fingers and toes and moved up her arms and legs until she felt like an electric current. *Is that it? That's not so bad.*

"Now, Kate. Just try not to be overexcited or too chatty." Pam steered her out to the pool deck. "You don't want to give yourself away."

Giddy, Kate clapped her hands together and said, "Well, let's get this thing going! Time to swim!" Was she being too loud? How could she turn it down? Her blood pumped, and her adrenaline flowed. The swim of her life lay just ahead. *And then I'll never take drugs again.* Her mind raced. *What have I done? Nope, don't go there. No regrets.*

Off the block like she'd been shot from a cannon, Kate gave it all she had. Her heart raced; her limbs tingled. The water felt even colder than usual on her flushed skin. She swam the whole race only taking a breath every five strokes, something she'd never done before.

After she made her turn and started on the last length of the race, she passed the other swimmers who hadn't made it to their turns yet. She would win for sure, and it looked good for setting the record—*but at what cost?*

She cleared any dark clouds from her mind and focused on the race. *Push, pull, stretch. Bam.* The race ended as fast as it began. The roar of the crowd pretty much confirmed that she'd set a new record. She ripped off her goggles and looked at the clock.

48.35! She would forever be a record-breaking swimmer. Her teammates, who had been standing at the end of the lane cheering her on, reached down into the pool and pulled her out. They hugged Kate and clapped her on the back. Everyone danced around her.

Coach Thompson came to offer her congratulations, tissue in hand. She pulled Kate into a tight embrace, too choked up to speak.

Her mom came down from the bleachers to hug her before she disappeared into the locker room. "Mom! Did you see that? I broke the record." Kate jumped up and down. "I did it, Mom! I did it! Do you think Dad saw?"

"Slow down, sweetheart. I can hardly understand you!" She laughed, shaking her head. "I'm so proud of you. That was amazing! And, yes, I'm sure your dad saw you." She choked on those last words.

Oops. Kate wished she hadn't asked about her dad at that moment—it made Mom sad. But Kate was sure glad to know that Mom believed that he had been watching. *But that means he probably saw me in the locker room.* She quickly dismissed that thought, allowing nothing to cloud her beautiful day.

Still, bubbling with excitement, Kate wanted to be with her team. "Mom, I know you drove a long way to see me swim, and I normally ride home with you. You probably won't want to drive home alone, but would you mind if I went back with the team? It's going to be tough to pull myself away from the celebration right now. I kind of want to hang out and celebrate. . . ." She screamed at herself to slow down but just couldn't.

"Okay, just relax." Mom laughed. "It's fine with me if you want to ride home on the bus. I think I would, too, if I were you." She hugged her daughter and looked deeply into her eyes. "I love you, Kate, and I'm so proud of you. I'll pick you up from school, and we'll celebrate together at home later."

"Thanks. Bye, Mom!" Kate kissed her and then skipped as she entered the locker room.

"There she is! The star of the show!" The whole team turned and clapped as Kate approached.

Grinning, she took a theatrical bow and said, "First I want to thank. . ."

"One. . .two. . .three. . . Hip, hip, hooray! Hip, hip, hooray! Hip, hip, hooray!" they cheered again for Kate as she climbed onto the bus. Her face reddened, not used to having all eyes on her—but she could get used to it.

Kate found an empty seat toward the back by Pam, Brittany, and Sandy. She got up, sat back down, got up again. After three times, Sandy pretended to pull her down and hold her there. "I'm not going to let you up until we get to the school."

"You might have to sit on her." Brittany laughed.

About ninety minutes later, amid the raucous laughter and chatter that had been going on for the whole drive, Kate noticed that Pam had gone strangely quiet. Catching Pam's eye, Kate mouthed, "What's wrong?"

Pam shook her head and pointed down at her open bag on the floor—the bag where Pam had hidden the bottle of pills.

Instantly, Kate feared the worst—*please don't let them be missing*. She questioned Pam with her eyes.

Pam just shook her head again and mouthed one word: "Gone."

Where could they be? What could she do? *If we get caught. . .*but she couldn't think about that. They had to solve the problem before the coach found the pills. They had to find them first. She stood to her feet to start her search, when she saw Coach Thompson standing there, waiting for everyone's attention.

"Kate, would you mind having a seat? I need

to talk to you guys."

Kate slumped into her seat and looked out the window, imagining her dreams fading away like the mountains they passed. She braced herself.

"Girls, without any problems, I want a simple answer. Whose are these?" Coach held up Pam's bottle. "Just take responsibility for them and tell me whose they are. And then we'll figure out who took them."

Coach stood there and looked from girl to girl for three full minutes before Pam spoke up. "The bottle's mine, Coach."

Without expression, Coach replied, "Thank you, Pam. Now, who took them?" She looked at each girl again.

Kate's insides were torn to shreds. She looked at her friends—if only she could talk to them. What if they didn't want her to confess and ruin the day for the whole team? There was no way to know. If she didn't confess, they'd probably hate her for leaving them to face the consequences alone. *I don't know what to do!* She sucked on her finger, which had started to bleed where she had bitten her nail too low. She panted her breaths and her heart raced—panic or drug induced?

"Girls, I'm going to ask you one more time.

Just once more. And if no one confesses, or if I don't believe that everyone who needs to has confessed, I'll just have to call the police. Who took these pills today? Raise your hand if you took one or more of these pills today."

Kate looked around as three hands went slowly into the air. The moment of truth. Pam and Brittany had their hands up, and so did Sandy. *Do the honorable thing and join them or try to fade into the background and avoid it? Now or never.* She didn't want to do it, but she didn't think she could live with herself if she didn't.

"Going once, going twice. . ."

Kate slipped her hand into the air.

Coach sighed and squeezed her eyes closed for a moment.

Kate wished she could shrink and disappear.

The bus pulled into the driveway of the school. "All right, you four who raised your hand, please stay on board the bus. Everyone else, you're free to go. But I'm going to give you all one more chance to join your teammates if you had any part in this. Don't let me find out later that you didn't come clean when you had this chance. Trust me, it would be much worse on you if I found out that way."

Everyone else filed off the bus. Coach

shrank as she lumbered behind them toward the door of the bus—her shoulders slumped and her head hung low. Kate wiped the moisture off the window with her sleeve and peered out. The swimmers met up with their parents, hugged them, climbed into their cars, and sped away—free. When they all pulled away, Coach approached the remaining parents who were obviously confused.

Watching the coach's back, Kate assumed by her head movement that she was talking. The parents listened intently, their faces blank, until. . . *Shock.* There it was. They knew.

Mom! Oh, no, she looks so disappointed. The face she'd studied her whole life. *How could I have done this to her?*

After what seemed like a lifetime, the group broke up and the parents made their way onto the bus. Two moms looked as though they'd been crying. Kate's mom sat across from her but didn't look at her. Kate sat in silence and waited. Awkwardly, fearfully, very much alone.

Finally, Coach addressed the group. "Folks. . ." She looked at the grief-stricken parents, most of whom hadn't spoken to their girls yet. "I know how difficult this must be for each of you. I'm at a loss myself." She looked down at her feet and rubbed her temples. "At this point, I can't tell you exactly what will happen. I'm going to have to talk to the administration on Monday. I will probably find out that I should have called the police,"—she looked back up at them—"but I'm not going to." She made eye contact with a couple of dads, who nodded. "By the time the school gets involved on Monday, I'm guessing that it will be too late for that or that they'll decide not to involve the authorities. . . . At least I hope that's what will happen."

She paused before continuing. "I can promise you that any awards, trophies, records, or times from today will be removed from the record and from your possession. I'm also pretty confident in saying that you'll be asked to leave the team." She had been holding back tears while she spoke, but at that last part, she choked on a sob.

What have we done? Kate felt sick. Drugs or grief—she couldn't say for sure. Her hands shook, and her stomach threatened revolt.

Coach wiped her eyes and continued. "As you can see, this is very hard on me. I'm going to have to think long and hard about what I've done or said to contribute to the level of pressure it would take to drive you girls to this." Looking each girl in the eye, their coach said,

"I'm just so glad you're all okay. I don't know what I'd have done if something happened to any one of you." Crying openly, she sat down.

Once they were sure that Coach had nothing else to say, they gathered their belongings. One by one they filed off the bus. No one said a word.

Chapter 11

STRIPPED

On Monday morning, Kate's steps slowed as she approached the school—her heart pounded, and her stomach churned. It would be bad. But no matter how bad it got at school, it couldn't even come close to how difficult it had been at home over the weekend. Kate shuddered as she thought back over the past few days. Silence. Home had been like a funeral parlor, except worse. At least at a funeral, people hugged each other and offered support as they grieved their loss.

Kate sat quietly during her first-period class. When would the bomb explode? The door creaked open. She peeked up from her book— not really wanting to look. A student with an OFFICE badge pinned to her shirt handed a note to the teacher. *This is it.* Kate closed her book and reached for her bag.

"Kate." The teacher held the note out. "It's for you."

The walk from her desk to the front of the classroom seemed much longer than usual. She felt all eyes on her, their heat boring holes in her back. *Has word already gotten around?* When she got back to her seat, she unfolded the note.

Kate Walker, come to the office with your books at 11:00.

Her heart sank. Two hours to wait—she just wanted it over with.

The morning passed like slow drips from a faucet. *Plink. Plink. Tick. Tock.* Finally, Kate's watch said 10:55—time to go. She grabbed her bags and a few books that she might need— they probably expected it to run long.

The secretary directed her to the conference room. Sunshine broke through the wall of windows at the back of the room. Kate looked down the long oak table and at everyone who sat around it. Pam and both of her parents, Brittany and her mom, Sandy and her dad, their coach, the principal, the school counselor and some silver-haired man in a navy blue suit and a yellow tie. *Uh-oh.* She took a seat next to her mom. Mom looked away.

The clock struck eleven o'clock, and Principal Coleman opened the meeting. She cleared her throat and tapped the edge of a stack of papers on the thick table. The noise made several people jump. "Well, I'm so sad we have to have this meeting, but we have no choice." She looked down and took a deep breath. Her eyes moved quickly down the sheet of handwritten notes that had been torn out of a spiral notebook and placed on top of her pile.

She pulled the second sheet out from her stack. "What I'm going to do first is read to you from this paper. It's a description of the events exactly as I understand they happened. I'd like you to listen and then, if the facts are straight, each student should sign the paper."

"Will we get copies of everything we sign?" Sandy's dad asked.

"Absolutely, Mr. Coble. Okay, here's what I have. . ."

Her words were lost on Kate—she couldn't hear through the roaring in her ears. The room buzzed just like the television did when the cable went out. She tried to focus on the words but couldn't. She watched the paper make its way around the table until it lay in front of her mom. Without moving her head, Mom covered it with her hand and slid it with a robotic motion toward Kate.

Kate scrawled her name on the page and then slipped lower in her seat.

"Okay, then. Mr. Stot, our district administrator, will take over from here." The principal dropped into her seat with a thud and exhaled, her part over.

"Thanks, Marsha." The man in the navy suit stood to address the group. "I'm going to keep this short because my job here is about the consequences. Parents, between yourselves, the counselor, and your kids' teachers, you'll have to deal with the moral issues." He pulled a padded brown-leather portfolio out of his briefcase and opened it on the table. Reading from a legal-sized sheet of paper, he said:

"Relating to the incidence of the possession of amphetamines and illegal drug use at a school-sponsored sporting event on November 29th, for the period of three days, Sandra Coble, Brittany Drummond, Pamela McSwain, and Kate Walker will be suspended from school. This suspension will be recorded on each student's permanent record. In addition, any medals won at the aforementioned event must be surrendered, and any times recorded will be void. Furthermore, participation on any sports team sanctioned by this school will be prohibited for a period of twelve months from this date."

Twelve months. Kate went weak at the thought of not swimming next season.

He cleared his throat and continued in his drone. "However, that twelve-month sports suspension can be reduced to six months by participation in a drug and alcohol abuse program. Information about such programs will be forthcoming, and participation will be monitored by Susan Moore, the school counselor."

It should take longer than fifteen minutes to lose her whole life—but that's exactly how long it took. She felt like this came out of nowhere—this stripping of everything important to her. What did she expect, though? Still, she just couldn't imagine how to move on from here—who would she be? What would it be like to return to school after a suspension? What would people at church say once word got around? *Mark!* Did he know already? She probably should have called him last night and told him herself, but she couldn't bring herself to do it.

"Are you coming?"

The first words her mom said to her all day. *Sigh.* Kate looked around in surprise to realize that the room had emptied. Her mom waited at the door, still not making eye contact. Grabbing her bag, Kate squeezed through the door past her, careful not to touch her.

They drove home in silence and then steered clear of each other for the afternoon. The tinkling of silverware at the dinner table grated on her like nails scratching a chalkboard. Kate opened her mouth to say something three different times, but her words just got stuck in her throat; and then, after dinner, her mom just left the room without a word. Kate didn't know how to move on from this. What if they couldn't? What if her mom had finally cracked under the weight of grief?

No way. Kate slapped her hands on the kitchen table and stood up. Her wooden chair wobbled back and almost toppled.

She marched into the family room, determined to set things right. "Mom, we need to talk." Kate sat on the arm of the sofa, blocking the television.

Mom didn't look at Kate. Instead, she shifted six inches to the right and kept watching TV.

"Mom, we seriously need to get past this."
Kate took in a slow breath and pulled from deep
within her gut to find what she needed to say
to reach her mom. "I'm—I'm—I'm so sorry,
Mom." The words unleashed her tears. "I really
screwed up. I don't even know what happened.
Something came over me, and I made a
spur-of-the-moment decision. I hardly even
considered not doing it. I was just overcome
with compulsion to just take the pill. I'd give
anything to go back, Mom. . . ."

"Why, Kate? Because you got caught? Is that
why you're sorry, why you wish you hadn't done
it?" Mom's eyes narrowed in anger.

Kate tried to stop crying. She deserved her
mom's rage. How could she convince her that
she truly regretted what she'd done?

"You know, Kate. I tried to stop you. I told
you something like this would happen. You
didn't listen to me. You figured you knew best
and your mom was just an old worrywart—out
of touch." She finally turned to look at her
daughter, making eye contact for the first time
in days. "Well, I was right, Kate. Now you're
in a whole heap of trouble, you've cost yourself
a fun and exciting experience and probably a
college scholarship. You've got a permanent

school record with a suspension on it, and you can never say that you didn't take illegal drugs." She stood and paced the room. "Illegal drugs, Kate. I can't believe it. And now you have to go to drug counseling, too—*you*, Kate. I don't get how this happened to you. Why couldn't you have listened to me?" She dropped to her knees at the edge of the sofa like when she prayed at the church altar.

"I did stop, Mom. . .when you told me no more. . .I did stop." *Please believe me.*

"No, Kate. That's where you're wrong. You stopped until it became too hard to keep your word." She bit her lip and shook her head. "Once things became too hard, you listened to someone else. What, does Pam love you more than me? Is she smarter than your simple old mom? Or did she just give you a way to do what you wanted to do all along?"

"I wish I could go back, Mom." Kate looked away and sighed.

"Did your friends know you're a Christian?"

Kate hung her head in shame. "No, Mom, not really."

Mom made eye contact with Kate. "Is your faith not as important to you as I thought it was?"

"No, Mom! Please don't think that. I screwed up. This doesn't define me. I made a mistake. Please don't make me out to be so bad, Mom." She walked to the window and stared out into the snowy night. "You know, Mom, I don't think I can ever really make you understand my motives and how I just got messed up. Everything you said is true. You're completely right. But there's nothing I can do now. I can't change anything about this situation. I can only change my thinking from now on."

"I'm sorry, Kate. You're right." Mom lifted her hands and shook her head. "We all make mistakes. You're going to have to give me some time to get over this. It's just so disappointing. And. . .and I miss your dad." Mom put her face in her hands and sobbed, her shoulders shaking with her grief. "He would have known what to do. No. . .this wouldn't have happened if he'd been around."

Unsure, Kate sat still for a moment. But even if Mom didn't want her comfort, Kate just couldn't sit by and watch her mom sob without going to her. She knelt on the floor next to her mom, their legs touching. Kate reached her arms out and pulled Mom to her.

Mom pressed her hands into her eyes, the tears leaking between her fingers like a breaking dam, and collapsed into Kate—months, years, of grief pouring out onto her daughter's shoulders.

The sun went down, but neither of them made a move to leave the now dark room. It had been years since they had held each other like this. Kate hadn't realized how much she hungered for the comfort of loving arms. Finally, they pulled apart and looked at each other. "I'm really sorry, Mom. I love you," Kate whispered.

"I love you, too, honey. I'm sorry, too."

Kate shook her head. "Why would you be sorry?"

"No, I really am sorry for making this so hard on you. You did the wrong thing. That's a fact. But I've done my share of wrong things." She blew her nose. "I guess, as a mom, I just want my little girl to avoid the hurt that comes from big mistakes. But it doesn't always work that way. I can't always protect you from everything. You're going to have to face the consequences of your decisions, Kate. But not alone. I'm here with you, for you. You, me, and Jesus—we make a pretty nice team." She smiled.

"I love you."

Kate threw her arms around her mom's neck one more time. "Thank you, Mom. I love you, too."

"Can we pray together?" Mom looked hopeful.

"I'd like nothing more." Kate smiled.

One broken relationship fixed; how many more to go?

Chapter 12

GRACE—A LEGAL DRUG

She dialed slowly, not quite ready to face the hurt she'd caused yet another loved one.

"Hello, Kate," Olivia answered with a short, clipped tone, enunciating the *t* so crisply that it felt like a slap.

Kate shrank away from the phone. She had messed everything up. Everything. "Liv. . ." She choked back the tears. "I'm. . .sorry. . . ." A sob welled in her throat and then overflowed. Her shoulders shook with her gut-wrenching sobs. She looked at the dripping phone and thought about just hanging it up, sure that Olivia wouldn't be on the other end when she got herself together anyway. But she just held on. And cried. *Jesus, please heal my friendship.*

When her tears slowed and her grief gave way to the promise of peace—at least inside— she took a few shuddering, cleansing breaths and placed the phone to her ear once again. "Liv?" she pleaded, desperate for acceptance.

"Kate? What on earth is going on? Talk to me." Her voice had softened, and she sounded just like the Olivia that she knew and loved— and needed.

"First, Liv, I need you to tell me you forgive me. Please. I've been a horrible fr–"

Olivia interrupted her. "It doesn't matter at all. You obviously went through something and got weird for whatever reason. I'm just glad you're back." She rushed her words. "But"—her tone grew more insistent—"you need to tell me what's going on."

Kate took a deep breath and grabbed her doodle pad. "Well it all started with a cup of coffee. . . ."

Olivia hardly said a word until Kate finished, and then she said the three words that Kate needed to hear more than anything: "I love you."

Feeling like a felon in an old movie, she might as well have been wearing a black-and-white striped jumpsuit when she walked into the school the first day after her suspension. She kept her head down as she walked down the hallway to her locker, sure everyone stared at her. *Just get through today. It will get easier.* Her head knew the truth, but her stomach didn't believe it.

What had she done? Everyone looked at her differently now.

Pam and Brittany saw her coming down the hall and immediately turned the other way.

"Don't mind them." Sandy came up behind her. "They aren't used to not getting their way. They don't have much use for you now that they know the real you. You're just finding out their true colors."

"Yeah, I guess so." Kate watched them walk away. "Maybe things will change in time."

"You never know." Sandy looked down and scuffed her shoe. "Hey, Kate. I was wondering . . .would it be okay if I went to church with you this Sunday?"

Kate's shoulders relaxed and she exhaled, relieved. "I would like nothing more. And I have another proposition for you. . . ."

"You guys have room up there for a singer?"

Kate walked down the aisle at the church. Mark and his buddies had arranged a practice for the band they decided to put together without Kate, if they had to. They hadn't talked to Kate about it since the "incident."

Mark beamed when he saw her coming toward them. "Room? As long as you check your big head at the door," he joked.

"Ha-ha, you're real funny, Mark." She looked at P.J., who had a cord wrapped around his hands, trying to set up the microphones, and Gabe, off to the side hooking up amplifiers. "How about you guys? Do you mind if I join you?" They stopped everything, shifted their weight, and didn't look at her. They certainly didn't look thrilled at the prospect of her joining the band. "Okay, let me have it, you guys. What's going on?"

"Well. . ." P.J. looked down at his shoe as he kicked at a piece of bright yellow tape on the stage. "It's just that we're concerned about you and aren't sure if it's a good time for you to do something like this. It's, well, it's a ministry. . . ," he trailed off and looked to Gabe.

"Kate, how are you doing with everything you have going on?" Gabe looked uncomfortable, too. "How do we know if you're. . .um. . .over everything?"

Ah, that's what they needed to know. "You're asking me whether or not I'm back on the straight and narrow?"

"Pretty much. I mean, it's kind of important," P.J. said, now behind the drums.

"Sure it is. The best way I can explain myself is to tell you what a wise soul said to me yesterday on the phone." Kate winked at Mark. "I'm like Peter. I screwed up. I didn't stand up for my faith, I didn't share it with anyone, and then I made a really bad decision." Kate walked up onto the stage and looked at each of them. "But also like Peter, Jesus not only forgives me for it, but He knew it would happen. He has guided me through it, healed my relationships, and taught me a lot of things because of it. So, yes, He and I are cool."

"Works for me." Gabe turned back to the sound equipment, satisfied to drop the subject.

"That's all I wanted to know." P.J. smiled and let out a sigh of relief.

"So, in other news, Mark and I have a proposition for you guys." Kate baited them.

"What's going on?" Gabe looked confused.

"Well, we've been rustling up the Christians we know from school, and we already talked to Pastor Rick. We want to start a little Bible study/prayer group before school on Tuesday mornings." As usual, Kate's words tumbled over each other when she got excited.

Mark jumped in. "Yeah, we're feeling like we need a boost to our faith, kind of like an encouragement to live it at school. It's too easy to separate church and school."

"What a great idea." P.J. thumped the bass drum. "Count me in."

"Me, too. I'm all for it." Gabe looked excited. "Maybe we could take turns leading it or something."

"That's the spirit. I'm really excited, you guys." Kate beamed. "It starts this coming Tuesday at seven thirty."

"Now, if there's nothing else, we have some music to play." Mark hopped up onto the stage.

"Well," P.J. said, "there *is* one other thing I want to know. What's the deal with you two already?" He pointed at Mark and Kate.

They both laughed and gazed at each other with the deep love of friendship. "Should we tell them?" Kate asked, batting her eyelashes at Mark.

"Yeah, I think it's time to break their hearts. Let 'em down easy, Kate."

"P.J., Mark and I are great friends. We've decided that we're just going to keep it that way for a while."

P.J. pretended to pull a knife out of his heart.

"We just don't want to ruin a great friendship by rushing, and we don't want to find ourselves in another situation we aren't prepared for. . . . Everything in His time is better anyway, right?"

Mark didn't take his eyes off Kate and added, "All in *His* time."

My Decision

I, *(include your name here)*, have read the story of Kate Walker and have learned from the choices she made and the consequences she faced. I promise to think before I act and, in all things, to choose God's will over mine.

Additionally,

- I will never take any legal substance that is offered to me by anyone other than a trusted adult.
- I will never take illegal drugs.
- I will guard my heart closely and not jump into a dating relationship before God says I'm ready.
- I will never be afraid to share my faith with others.

Please pray the following prayer:

Father God, I know that I am a blank slate. Please let the lessons that I learned as I read about Kate imprint on the slate of my heart.

Help me to honor my parents by making right choices and avoiding questionable situations. I want to commit to You now that I'll avoid any use of illegal drugs—please help me do that when the time comes and I'm feeling the pressure.

Also, please forgive me for the times when I haven't shared my faith with others. Help me to have the strength to do it even when it's difficult.

I know that You have everything under control, so I submit to Your will. Amen.

Congratulations on your decision! Please sign this contract signifying your commitment. Have someone you trust, like a parent or a pastor, witness your choice.

_____

Signed

_____

Witnessed by

Check it out!

For information on the latest Scenarios
books, great giveaways, girl talk, and more
visit scenariosforgirls.com!

SCENARIOS FOR GIRLS

Book 1: TRUTH OR DARE
Lindsay Martin is faced with a tough choice: Does she give in to peer pressure and make her friends happy or does she do what she knows is right—even if it means losing her friends forever?

Book 2: ALL THAT GLITTERS
Drew Daniels finally has what she thought she wanted—popularity and a cute boyfriend. But now she's faced with choosing between her boyfriend and doing what's right.

Book 3: MAGNA
Molly Jacobs isn't sure what she should do: Should she follow through with stealing clothes for her friends from Magna—the trendy girls' clothing store where she works? Or should she do what she knows is right, even if it means losing her newfound popularity?

Available wherever books are sold.